Today's Debates

REPRODUCTIVE TECHNOLOGY

Indispensable or Problematic?

Erin L. McCoy and Jon Sterngass

Cavendish Square
New York

Published in 2020 by Cavendish Square Publishing, LLC
243 5th Avenue, Suite 136, New York, NY 10016

First Edition

Library of Congress Cataloging-in-Publication Data

Names: Sterngass, Jon, author. | McCoy, Erin L., author.
Title: Reproductive technology : indispensable or problematic? / Jon Sterngass and Erin L. McCoy.
Description: First edition. | New York : Cavendish Square, 2020. |
Series: Today's debates | Audience: Grades 7 to 12. | Includes bibliographical references and index. |
Identifiers: LCCN 2018057891 (print) | LCCN 2018059375 (ebook) |
ISBN 9781502644855 (ebook) | ISBN 9781502644848 (library bound) | ISBN 9781502644831 (pbk.)
Subjects: LCSH: Human reproductive technology—Moral and ethical aspects—Juvenile literature. |
Genetic engineering—Moral and ethical aspects—Juvenile literature. |
Bioethics—Juvenile literature. | Medical ethics—Juvenile literature.
Classification: LCC RG133.5 (ebook) | LCC RG133.5 .S7525 2020 (print) | DDC 176/.2—dc23
LC record available at https://lccn.loc.gov/2018057891

Editorial Director: David McNamara
Copy Editor: Michele Suchomel-Casey
Associate Art Director: Alan Sliwinski
Designer: Christina Shults
Production Coordinator: Karol Szymczuk
Photo Research: J8 Media

The photographs in this book are used by permission and through the courtesy of:
Cover, Ted Horowitz/Corbis/Getty Images; p. 4 CREATISTA/Shutterstock.com; p. 8 Monkey Business Images/Shutterstock.com; p. 12 Nattle/Shutterstock.com; p. 16 Subhash Sharma/Polaris/Newscom; p. 17 Nevodka/Shutterstock.com; p. 21 Bain News Service/PhotoQuest/Getty Images; p. 26 Rena Schild/Shutterstock.com; p. 28 Erika Sandtelices/AFP/Getty Images; p. 37 Jack Guez/AFP/Getty Images; p. 38 Jonas Gratzer/LightRocket/Getty Images; p. 42 Mahmud Hams/AFP/Getty Images; p. 46 https://www.nlm.nih.gov/hmd/frankenstein/frank_celluloid.html/ HYPERLINK "https://www.nlm.nih.gov/hmd/frankenstein/frank_celluloid.html/File"Pennsylvania State University Libraries/F HYPERLINK "https://www.nlm.nih.gov/hmd/frankenstein/frank_celluloid.html/File"ile: Criminal brains.jpg/Wikimedia Commons/Public Domain; p. 51 AP Photo/Joey Ivansco; p. 53 FPG/Hulton Archive/Getty Images; pg. 54 Jason O. Watson/Historicalmarkers.org/Alamy Stock Photo; p. 60 Zhang Wei/China News Service/VCG/Getty Images; p. 65 Vishal Bhatnagar/NurPhoto/Getty Images; p. 70 vchal/Shutterstock.com; p. 74 Yvette Mari Dostatni/Chicago Tribune/MCT/Getty Images; p. 79 Hulton Archive/Getty Images; p. 80 BSIP/UIG/Getty Images; p. 89 AP Photo/The Canadian Press, Jonathan Hayward; p. 91 AP Photo/The Topeka Capital-Journal, Mike Burley; p. 94 Gary Lee/UPPA/ZUMA Press; p. 97 Carolyn Van Houten/The Washington Post/Getty Images; p. 98 Spencer Platt/Getty Images; p. 103 Zbigniew Bzdak/Chicago Tribune/MCT/Getty Images; p. 106 Encyclopaedia Britannica/UIG/Getty Images;

Printed in the United States of America

CONTENTS

INTRODUCTION

Around the world, an estimated fifty million couples face problems with infertility. Defined as the inability to conceive a child after at least twelve months of trying, infertility can affect both men and women, but in many cultures, women are often blamed for a couple's inability to have children. "Our culture demands that, for a woman to be socially acceptable, she should have at least one biological child," one person from Kenya told the Maternal Health Task Force, a global organization of health workers, researchers, and policymakers. Those who don't have children can sometimes be socially ostracized or even abused. Even so, when a couple wants a child, they both often suffer a great deal of emotional pain at not being able to conceive.

Many men and women have found a solution to the problem of infertility in the development of increasingly sophisticated reproductive technologies. These are techniques used to

Opposite: As access to new and innovative reproductive technologies grows, countless couples who once may have had trouble conceiving are now able to have children.

overcome infertility, to increase fertility, or to influence or choose certain genetic characteristics of children. These medical advances thrill the world with the possibility of the elimination of disease and the ability to provide a better future for humanity. However, they also create anxiety about the creation of "designer babies" and clones, as well as the risk that these benefits of scientific progress will be available mainly to affluent people in developed countries.

The debate around each of these reproductive technologies may vary significantly throughout the world as a variety of cultures struggle to integrate them into their societies. In this book, we will primarily investigate the controversies around such technologies in the United States.

Infertility and Its Causes

About 85 to 90 percent of all couples will get pregnant within one year, if they are actively trying to do so, according to the US Department of Health and Human Services. However, twelve or thirteen in every one hundred couples in the United States passes this twelve-month mark, and 10 percent of women of childbearing age have trouble either getting pregnant or remaining pregnant.

About one-third of these cases are the result of fertility problems in men and one-third of fertility problems in women. The remaining one-third may be caused by a mixture of problems or may have underlying causes that have not been identified.

In women, such issues might stem from hormone problems or a blockage in the fallopian tubes, through which a woman's egg must pass to enter the uterus and begin a pregnancy. Less common causes might include physical issues with or tumors within the uterus—the womb that holds a baby as it is growing. Certain activities or life events, too, may reduce a woman's chance of getting pregnant. These include smoking or drinking alcohol.

In men, fertility problems can result if the body makes too few sperm. The sperm is a male reproductive cell that fertilizes the egg in a woman's body. Likewise, if the tubes through which sperm travel are blocked, a man will not be able to deliver sperm to a woman's egg. Smoking, alcohol and drug use, and being older than forty can cause or worsen fertility problems in men.

One of the primary methods for increasing a couple's chances of conceiving is to have intercourse, or sex, near the time of ovulation. Ovulation—when a woman's body releases eggs from the ovaries—occurs about every twenty-eight days. When such strategies don't work, however, couples may seek out other options.

The Debate

Among the new reproductive techniques that have emerged in recent decades are artificial insemination, sperm and egg donation, in vitro fertilization, preimplantation genetic diagnosis, and amniocentesis.

Each type of modern reproductive technology brings a range of ethical issues. Each provokes controversies involving the boundaries of government control, private choice, religious belief, and parental wishes. Some of these issues have been debated for many years in regards to child adoption. Others are relatively new.

Reproductive technology is moving so quickly that many important social, ethical, and legal considerations are lagging behind. Who should regulate the new technologies, and how should they be regulated? To what degree, if any, should market forces control who has access to new scientific discoveries? What are the rights and obligations of the various parties, such as sperm and egg donors, the children born through reproductive technology, and parents who choose these techniques?

The international community is only beginning to answer such questions. It was not until 2015 that the first International Summit on Human Genome Editing convened. At this conference, attendees opted for a voluntary moratorium—or temporary ban—on genome editing until deeper ethical discussions had taken place.

Chapter One

REPRODUCTIVE TECHNOLOGY TODAY

When a couple is having trouble conceiving a child, or when a single person wants to be a parent, they have many more resources at their disposal than they would have had even thirty years ago. Reproductive technologies and methods have advanced by leaps and bounds in recent decades. Let's take a look at the variety of approaches that people use to conceive today.

Donation of Sperm

One of the more "low-tech" forms of reproductive technology is sperm donation, in which a man donates his semen in order to engender a child in a woman

Opposite: Donated sperm is held in frozen storage at a sperm bank. Sperm can be donated to women or couples seeking to conceive.

who is not the man's sexual partner. Originally, private doctors used sperm donation to help couples overcome male fertility problems, such as low sperm count. Since 1990, however, the technique often has been used by single women, as well as lesbian and queer couples, as a way to have children.

Most pregnancies achieved by sperm donation are begun by means of artificial insemination. A sperm donor may donate his sperm to women through a clinic or sperm bank. On the other hand, he can use a "sperm agency," which makes private arrangements between sperm donors and recipient women. In the last two decades, sperm donation has become extremely common. Agencies offer catalogs of donors directly to would-be parents, as well as photos and audio and video recordings.

The typical sperm donor in the United States is anonymous, meaning that his identity is not revealed to the recipient. Doctors require potential donors to undergo a battery of physical tests and to provide their medical history. In the United States, sperm donors receive payment, usually between $50 and $200. The fresh sample is then processed and frozen in several small vials. Following a quarantine period, the samples are thawed and used to impregnate women.

The number of children fathered by a single donor can vary. A sperm bank may impose its own limits. However, some American donors may produce large numbers of children. Outside of the United States, most countries limit the number of children born from one donor.

Sometimes, donors and recipients arrange donations privately. Recipients may approach a friend, obtain the name of a private donor by advertising, or find a donor on a website. Private donations may not cost the recipients anything, but they carry greater risks associated with any unscreened body fluid contact. In most states, anonymous donors to a sperm bank enjoy certain legal protections that are not always available to personal donors. A personal donor, if traced, can be considered by the courts to be the legal father of each child produced by his sperm.

Although there is no official count of donor-conceived children, one estimate is that one million Americans are the biological children of sperm donors—mostly by anonymous fathers—with about thirty thousand to sixty thousand more born each year.

In Vitro Fertilization

Since 1990, sperm donation has often been linked with in vitro fertilization, known by the acronym IVF. "In vitro" literally means "in glass," as in a test tube. (A related term, "in vivo," means "in a living organism.")

Because an IVF procedure consists of several steps over a two-week period, it is usually described as a "cycle" of treatments instead of a single procedure. An IVF cycle begins when doctors give a woman a series of hormone injections to stimulate the ovaries to produce ten or more eggs (ova, or oocytes). The eggs are removed surgically and fertilized with donor sperm in a laboratory. Doctors then transfer some of the resulting embryos into a woman's uterus. Several eggs are usually implanted because of the possibility that some of the eggs will fail to develop. If the procedure is successful, nine months later, a baby is born. Children conceived through IVF are sometimes popularly referred to as "test-tube babies."

The first successful human pregnancy achieved through IVF occurred in 1977 when gynecologist Patrick Steptoe and research physiologist Robert Edwards pioneered the technique. On July 25, 1978, the conception resulted in the world's first IVF baby—Louise Brown, born in Manchester, England. The first

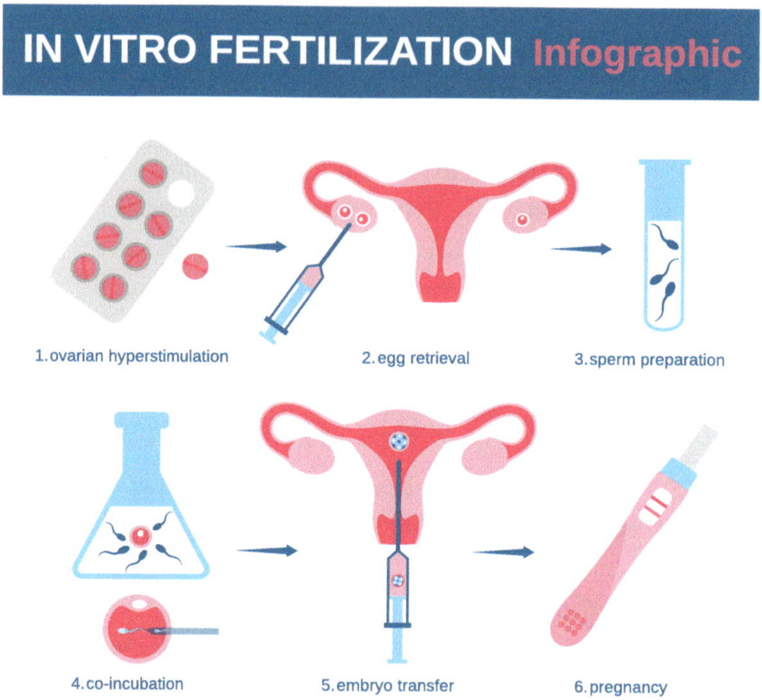

The process of in vitro fertilization, from the removal of the eggs to their insemination to their reinsertion in the woman's body, is shown.

successful IVF in the United States was performed in 1981. In October 2010, Edwards received the Nobel Prize in Medicine for the development of in vitro fertilization.

IVF is often used by women who cannot ovulate or whose eggs might transmit a harmful genetic condition. This technology also overcomes the problem of scarred, damaged, or blocked fallopian tubes, which prevent sperm from reaching the eggs and the eggs from reaching the uterus. It can even allow men with low sperm counts to conceive because their sperm samples can be concentrated and deposited right next to the ripe eggs.

A variation of the IVF procedure involves a specialized technique known as intracytoplasmic sperm injection (ICSI). In ICSI, doctors inject a single sperm directly into the woman's egg. This technique allows a man whose sperm have proved to be too weak or too few to fertilize his partner's eggs.

Sometimes embryos are transferred to the uterus on the third day after conception. Other doctors prefer to wait until the embryo becomes a blastocyst—usually between days five and eight. A blastocyst is a spherical mass of about 150 cells. It consists of an outer embryo lining, which will form the placenta, and an inner cell mass, which will become the fetus. The inner cell mass also produces embryonic stem cells.

The number of embryos that should be created or transferred during an IVF cycle is open to debate. The mainstream position is that there is no need to transfer more than four embryos per IVF cycle for optimal results. Transferring four embryos rather than one or two increases the probability that pregnancy will occur. Many researchers believe that transferring more than four embryos causes too many multiple pregnancies, which increases the possibility of other complications.

In the United States, the IVF process typically (but not always) generates more embryos than will be implanted. People using IVF must then decide about the status of the embryos that were not implanted: whether to donate them for use in stem cell research, donate them to someone else, freeze and store them (where they will remain viable for at least twenty-five years, or even longer), or discard them. Every one of these choices presents ethical and legal dilemmas. In some countries, such as Germany, the law regulates fertility clinics and prohibits doctors from fertilizing more eggs than will be implanted at any one time.

The success rate of an IVF cycle depends on many factors. In the United States in 2015, the rate of live births for each IVF cycle started was about 38 percent for women under thirty-five. However, the figure dropped to about 14 percent for women aged forty-one or forty-two, and 7 percent for women aged forty-three or forty-four.

IVF is an expensive procedure, costing between $11,000 and $12,000 for each cycle. What's more, many women will undergo multiple cycles of IVF, since there is only a 21.3 percent chance of having a full-term, normal birth for every cycle. This means that the procedure is used mainly by the well-to-do and is not accessible to the poor. This is especially the case in the United States, where health insurance often does not pay for fertility treatment (although several states do mandate insurance coverage for fertility treatment).

In the twenty-first century, IVF has become the last hope for most fertility problems. About 1–2 percent of babies born every year in the United States are via IVF, totaling 61,740 births in 2012, the latest year for which figures are available.

Preimplantation Genetic Diagnosis

In the famous novel *Brave New World* (1932), author Aldous Huxley imagined a future world in which natural reproduction no longer existed. Instead, children were created ("decanted") and raised in factory-like institutions known as Hatcheries and Conditioning Centers. At their creation, the children were divided into five castes to fill preset social and economic roles. Huxley's predictions, initially scorned as far-fetched, seemed a little less so after doctors completed the first preimplantation genetic diagnosis procedure in 1988 at Hammersmith Hospital in London.

Preimplantation genetic diagnosis, also known as PGD, is a form of prenatal diagnosis. Doctors use the PGD procedure to screen embryos before any undeveloped cell mass is implanted as part of IVF treatment. This practice allows parents to select one or more specific embryos before initiating a pregnancy. Doctors remove a single cell from the embryo for a biopsy and test its DNA for information. For couples or individuals with a high risk of transmitting an inherited condition, embryo screeners look for markers for specific genetic disorders or chromosomal abnormalities such as hemophilia, cystic fibrosis, Huntington's chorea, or sickle-cell disease. Parents may then choose to implant an embryo that is free of the genetic disease, if such an embryo is available.

The PGD procedure is safe but not entirely risk-free. The screening of embryos is not foolproof, either, and there is always a chance of missing targeted genetic disorders. However, the use of PGD arouses tremendous controversy, horrifying some commentators because of a perceived resemblance to the genetic manipulation in *Brave New World*. For example, some couples have been using PGD to choose a child of a particular sex.

Controversy over the use of PGD has prompted some countries to enact laws regulating the procedure. In Germany, the Embryo Protection Act of 1990 completely prohibited the use of PGD, though it is now allowed when screening for serious genetic defects. Many other countries permit PGD, but their governments control its usage. One such regulatory agency is Great Britain's Human Fertilisation and Embryology Authority (HFEA), a government body that regulates fertility treatment and embryo research and authorizes only limited use of PGD. However, in the United States the use of PGD is unregulated.

Surrogate Mothers

The ability to fertilize a human egg in a glass dish made it possible to combine gametes from any man and woman and implant the fertilized egg into any other woman. IVF made it possible for any woman with a functioning uterus to carry and deliver a baby for someone else. In this way, IVF separated the roles of birth mother and genetic mother.

Surrogate mothers, hired by people from around the globe to carry their children, talk and share photos at the Surrogate House in Gujarat, India.

This raised the possibility of women who might choose to be employed as surrogate mothers, also known as gestational carriers. The surrogate carries a child who will be raised by another woman. Between 1999 and 2013, 18,400 babies were born to surrogates in the United States, 53.4 percent of whom were twins or higher-order multiple births, according to the Centers for Disease Control and Prevention (CDC). Sixteen percent of surrogate mothers, in these cases, were not residents of the United States.

Surrogacy was a popular solution for infertility in the 1980s, but as IVF improved, surrogacy faded from view. However, surrogacy is still an option for some individuals and couples—if, for example, the woman can neither produce viable eggs nor carry a pregnancy to term. Some gay or queer male couples also use surrogacy in order to have a child fathered by one partner. They need an egg and a uterus, and there are women willing to provide both.

A major problem that may occur during surrogacy is that hormonal changes during pregnancy can produce a "maternal instinct" in the pregnant woman. That is, a surrogate mother who has given birth may become reluctant to fulfill her contract by giving up the child. In general, courts have ruled that the surrogate mother is allowed to renege rather than follow through in fulfilling her contract. However, governments have sometimes stepped in when the welfare of the child is at stake.

A surrogate mother usually signs a contract to provide the service and to allow the adoption of the baby upon birth. In exchange, all her medical costs are covered and she is paid between $23,000 and $45,000; higher fees are paid to experienced surrogates. Technically, the payment is for the donor's time, not for the child itself. The fee paid for surrogacy, like the fee for egg donation, is the source of great controversy. Much of Europe bans the practice, and many states refuse to recognize surrogacy contracts. However, other states have legalized the practice and regulate it.

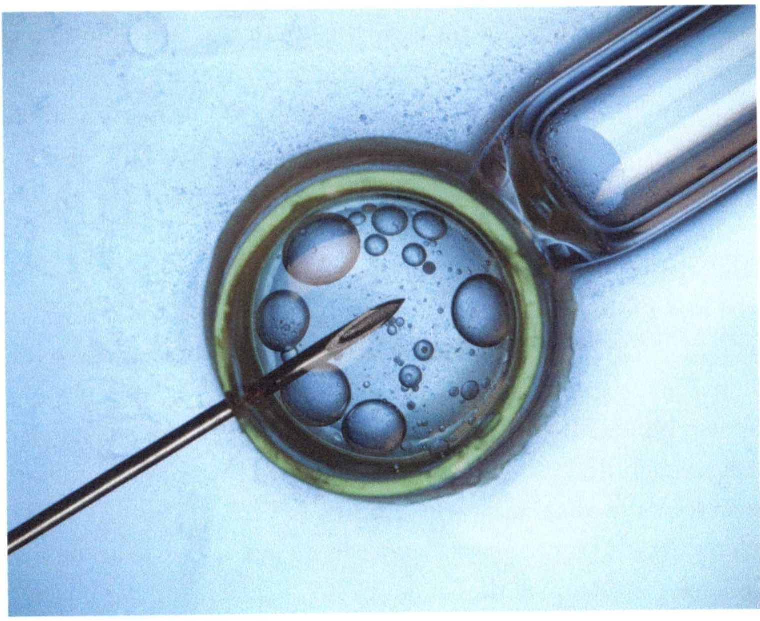

An egg is implanted with sperm during the in vitro fertilization process.

Donation of Eggs

The popularity of IVF led to the possibility of egg donation, the process by which a woman provides several eggs for an act of assisted reproduction in which no additional participation from her is contemplated. It is also possible to freeze eggs for future use, a process known as oocyte cryopreservation.

Egg donation can have serious undesirable side effects for the donor, including abdominal swelling, mood swings, and hot flashes. The most significant risk is ovarian hyperstimulation syndrome, which can cause abdominal pain, nausea, diarrhea, shortness of breath, and sometimes even life-threatening ailments. The risk to an egg donor, as well as the time involved, explains why the cost of donated eggs is considerably higher than donated sperm.

The first child conceived through egg donation was born in 1984 in Australia. Since then, more than one hundred thousand babies have been born worldwide through this procedure. This number will probably continue to grow because more women are waiting longer to begin their families and because there will be more women who survive cancer but lose the function of their ovaries.

At first, most egg donors were infertile women who were undergoing IVF and had produced extra eggs. However, in the late 1980s, fertility clinics began recruiting donors through newspaper and magazine advertisements. Soon, freestanding egg donation programs arrived. These brokerages function much like sperm banks. They recruit and screen prospective egg donors, help match donors with appropriate recipients, and coordinate everyone's medical care with a fertility center. The procedural change made pregnancy through egg donation easy to arrange as long as a woman had the money or her health insurance covered the procedure.

Some countries have either banned egg donation completely or made it very difficult to pursue. Others have banned payments for egg donors. However, the practice is common in the United States. Many foreign residents come to the United States for human eggs; this is known as fertility tourism.

Popular opinion seems to be mixed on the subject of egg donation. Some people wonder whether it is ethical for one woman to use hormones beyond what her body naturally produces and undergo a surgical procedure to help another woman create a child that is not biologically hers and that will never know his or her genetic mother. However, women who donate eggs say they do not see the egg as their child. They compare the egg donation to giving blood, a valuable part of a person's body that can benefit someone else without undue inconvenience to the donor. Other women say they would never consent to give away their genetic material and are astonished that not everyone feels the same way.

Stem Cell Research

In theory, stem cell research is not a procedure related to reproduction. Since, however, stem cells are often derived from early-stage embryos, and since these embryos are usually the product of IVF, the issue of stem cell research has become intertwined with the topic of assisted reproductive technology. People who believe that embryos are entitled to the same rights as human beings consider procedures that derive stem cells from embryos to be equivalent to murder.

Stem cells are unspecialized cells that renew themselves through cell division. Scientists work mainly with stem cells of two different kinds: embryonic stem cells and adult stem cells. In a three- to five-day-old embryo, stem cells in developing tissues turn into specialized cells that make up the heart, lung, skin, and other tissues. In some adult tissues, such as bone marrow,

Prenatal Tests and Monitoring

Amniocentesis and ultrasound are two older forms of reproductive technology that continue to raise ethical questions. During pregnancy, a water-like substance called amniotic fluid surrounds the fetus. Analysis of this fluid can provide information about fetal health. Doctors and researchers first used it to try to diagnose genetic disease in 1956.

Amniocentesis is now a common prenatal test often performed between the fifteenth and eighteenth week of pregnancy. A doctor uses a fine needle to remove a small amount (less than one ounce) of amniotic fluid, and technicians then perform laboratory tests on the extracted material. Although amniocentesis does not identify all possible birth defects, it can detect Down syndrome, sickle-cell disease, cystic fibrosis, muscular dystrophy, Tay-Sachs disease, and spina bifida. The procedure, which does present a small risk for both the mother and her baby, is accurate about 99 percent of the time.

Doctors are usually guided in performing amniocentesis by ultrasound. Ultrasound is also used to check on the health of the baby, independent of amniocentesis procedures. This imaging procedure uses high-frequency sound waves to visualize internal organs and produce moving images of the fetus's body. Originally used as sonar to track submarines, the medical version of the procedure was first used on patients in the 1950s.

Because ultrasound is often performed with amniocentesis, the test may indirectly detect birth defects. Ultrasound and amniocentesis are also the most accurate way to determine a fetus's sex. In some nations, this has led to ethical controversies because some prospective parents who wanted male children have chosen to abort female fetuses.

muscle, and brain, stem cells create replacements for cells that are lost through normal use, injury, or disease.

Because stem cells have such valuable qualities, stem cell research has the potential for finding a cure or treatment for such conditions as breast and prostate cancer, juvenile and adult-onset diabetes, leukemia, Parkinson's disease, Alzheimer's disease, spinal cord injuries, and Huntington's chorea. It also has the potential to repair human tissues, nerve cells, and skin cells. An estimated 5.7 million people in the United States suffer from Alzheimer's disease, and another one million are projected to have Parkinson's disease by 2020, with about sixty thousand new cases diagnosed every year. More than ten million people around the globe suffer from this debilitating disease. If stem cell research can help treat even some of these people, the demand for it will remain tremendous.

In 1998, researchers first isolated stem cells from human embryos and grew the cells in the laboratory. The embryos used in these studies had been created in an IVF procedure. When they were no longer needed for that purpose, they were donated for research with the informed consent of the donor.

People who believe abortion is ethically acceptable have few problems with stem cell research because they do not believe that a three- to five-day-old embryo is a person. Furthermore, they point out that IVF embryos, if not used for stem cell research, would be destroyed—a worse fate for them, considering how many people stem cell research has the potential to help. However, people who believe that personhood begins at conception insist that harvesting stem cells from embryos is unethical and immoral. Because they believe killing embryos is a form of abortion, they object to using stem cells, even from the thousands of frozen embryos that are stored in reproductive clinics, where they lose their viability as years pass.

Birth Control and Prevention

In a sense, many modern forms of contraception and abortion are also a form of reproductive technology, only their aim is to prevent the conception or birth of a child rather than to encourage it. The issue of abortion intersects with procedures such as IVF and PGD, which sometimes create more embryos than are needed. The ultimate fate of these embryos has become linked, especially in the United States, with the debate over whether an embryo is a person and whether destroying it or using it for research constitutes murder.

People have used abortion and birth control methods for thousands of years to reduce the likelihood of pregnancy or childbirth. Before the Industrial Revolution, birth control technology consisted mainly of condoms for men, made from linen or the lining of animal intestines. Women tried douches or the insertion into the vagina of substances or devices known as "pessaries" to block or kill sperm. As a last resort, if a child was conceived, abortion-inducing plants were also used. At best, these female contraceptive methods succeeded only part of the time.

Contraception

The development of rubber vulcanization in 1839 helped the development of the contraceptive industry, producing condoms (sometimes called "rubbers") for men, as well as douching syringes, vaginal sponges, diaphragms, and cervical caps for women. However, in 1873, the US Congress passed the Comstock Act. This law prohibited the distribution of advertisements and information about birth control, as well as the devices themselves, and allowed for the confiscation of any birth control products sold through the mail. This made innovative birth control methods extremely difficult to access.

Margaret Sanger (*right*) is pictured at a New York City clinic in 1916. The clinic was closed nine days after opening, and Sanger, a birth control activist, was jailed on obscenity charges.

Beginning in the 1880s, increasing medical knowledge led to the use of surgical sterilization as a form of birth control. Tubal ligation, first performed in 1881, is a procedure in which a woman's fallopian tubes are cut or tied off, preventing sperm from fertilizing eggs. Doctors performed the first vasectomy, or male sterilization, in the late 1890s. In this minor surgical procedure, a part of the tubes carrying the sperm from the testicles is removed and the ends are sealed.

Before the 1960s, American doctors would perform surgical sterilization for medical reasons only; voluntary surgical sterilization was not even legal in most of the United States. A half-century later, however, about seven hundred thousand tubal sterilizations and six hundred thousand vasectomies were being performed in the United States each year. In addition, an estimated two hundred million couples worldwide have used surgical sterilization as a method of contraception.

The modern birth control movement in the United States dates to 1916, when Margaret Sanger opened the first American birth control clinic in Brooklyn, New York. For the next fifty years, American reformers fought to make birth control freely available to people who wanted to use it.

In the 1960s, the development and mass production of effective birth control pills for women heralded a new era in contraception. Birth control pills contain synthetic hormones, which prevent ovulation by mimicking the way real estrogen and progestin work in a woman's body. No new eggs are released by a woman using birth control pills because the hormones "trick" her body into believing she is already pregnant.

At the time of the introduction of birth control pills, many states still had laws prohibiting the use of contraception. In 1965, the US Supreme Court ruled in the case *Griswold v. Connecticut* that a Connecticut law prohibiting the use of contraceptives violated a person's "right to marital privacy." In 1972, the Supreme

Court case of *Eisenstadt v. Baird* expanded the right to privacy to include the possession and use of contraceptives by unmarried couples. According to 2011–2013 data from the CDC, 61.7 percent of American women between the ages of fifteen and forty-four reported the use of some form of contraception to prevent pregnancy. What's more, "Nearly all women use contraception at some point in their lifetimes," the CDC confirmed.

Abortion

The Griswold case would have major consequences for American reproductive politics. In 1973, in the case of *Roe v. Wade*, the US Supreme Court declared that a woman's constitutionally protected right to privacy included the right to obtain an abortion. Since that time, the right of a woman to choose whether to carry a pregnancy to term or not has become one of the central rights protected by the US Constitution.

Since *Roe v. Wade*, doctors have performed more than forty-five million legal abortions in the United States. In 2015, the latest year for which data was available, 638,169 legal abortions were performed in the United States, according to the CDC. The majority of those receiving abortions were women in their twenties. The most common method, vacuum aspiration, was pioneered in China in 1958 and perfected in the United States in the 1970s. Vacuuming the contents of the uterus with a syringe replaced the older dilation and curettage method (also known as D&C) in which the walls of the uterus were scraped with a hard metal instrument called a curette.

Although the moral controversy and debate over abortion is beyond the scope of this book, the debate greatly affects many ethical decisions on reproductive technology. In general, proponents of the position popularly known as "pro-life" argue that a blastocyst, a human embryo, and a fetus are all human beings with a right to live; they consider any abortion equivalent

Pro-choice and pro-life activists demonstrate outside the US Supreme Court on June 27, 2016.

to murder. They point out that women who do not want to keep a child, or feel they cannot keep it, can always put the child up for adoption. Why commit infanticide, they ask, when other parents out there may be eagerly awaiting a child to adopt?

In contrast, supporters of the position popularly identified as "pro-choice" argue that a woman has certain inalienable reproductive rights, especially the choice of whether or not to carry a pregnancy to full term. They also point out that abortion supports socioeconomic equality by ensuring that women who may be charged with the primary caretaker role have the same choices as men, who are often free of the consequences of an unwanted pregnancy. Likewise, individuals without the money or resources to raise a child are more likely to have a chance to rise out of poverty without one. They point out that many people find abortion personally and practically necessary in some cases. "People will come into my office in tears and say they've been against abortion their whole lives," said one fertility specialist, "but they'll make an exception for themselves."

The American Society for Reproductive Medicine (ASRM) has tried to forge a compromise position in the polarized debate over abortion. The ASRM has stated that "fertilized eggs and preimplantation embryos, while not people or moral subjects in their own right, should not be treated like any other human tissue. Because of their potential to be implanted and bring forth a new person, they deserve 'special respect.'" However, this compromise position seems to satisfy few people on either side of the debate.

The many reproductive technologies available today have aided many individuals who may not have been able to have a child just a few decades ago. Many have heralded them as triumphs of innovation and a boon to humanity. Others, however, point to potential ethical dilemmas surrounding these methods—dilemmas that will evolve and change alongside the technologies themselves.

CAMINATA
Huellas de ternura
POR EL
AMOR
#UnPasoporMiFamilia
POR LA
TERNURA

Chapter Two

THE RELIGIOUS VIEWPOINT

How does one define human life? Is an embryo a human? A ten-week-old fetus? Does a fetus become a human being at some particular moment when it is still in the womb, or does it only become human when it is born? All of these questions are central to ethical questions surrounding reproductive technology today, especially for people whose religious beliefs might conflict with these methods. For many, the legalization of abortion in the United States in 1973 brought these issues into sharp focus.

The deliberate creation of embryos by artificial means is the basis of almost all reproductive technologies. In vitro fertilization (IVF), the most common fertility treatment, results not only in the hoped-for baby

Opposite: Members of the Catholic Church demonstrate against abortion in the Dominican Republic in 2018. The Dominican Republic is one of twenty-six countries where abortion is illegal in all cases.

(when successful), but often in the creation of extra embryos. These embryos are usually put into long-term storage and either used when an opportunity arises or, eventually, discarded and destroyed. In other cases, they are used for research. The status of these embryos is the subject of a great deal of philosophical controversy in the twenty-first century.

Many people derive their ethics from their religious upbringing. Billions of people around the world are followers of ancient religions such as Christianity, Judaism, Islam, Hinduism, and Buddhism, which all predate modern science. The scriptures and other teachings of these religions, which people consult for guidance, have nothing specifically to say about IVF or preimplantation genetic diagnosis (PGD). Nonetheless, many people look to religious leaders for direction on these difficult ethical questions. Not surprisingly, religions vary widely in their views of the ethics of reproductive technology. Even within a religious tradition, there is often dispute about what constitutes the proper ethical choice.

At one extreme, many people of various religious faiths regard embryos as human beings from the moment of conception, defined as the instant at which a sperm penetrates an egg. They see embryos as human lives with the same rights as all other humans. According to this view, the deliberate destruction of embryos is the same as abortion, and both are acts of murder. People who hold this view often oppose almost every modern reproductive technology. As US senator Sam Brownback of Kansas expressed, "A human embryo … is a human being just like you and me and it deserves the same respect that our laws give to all of us."

At the other extreme, some people—both religious and nonreligious—view a blastocyst as a clump of cells with only the *potential* to become a human baby. They believe that personhood begins in the later stages of fetal development. People who hold this view often accept abortion up to a certain time limit. They also support the use of reproductive technology depending on the situation.

The Catholic Perspective

An estimated 1.28 billion people are followers of Roman Catholicism. The sheer number of people who belong to this denomination, and the fact that the church applies the same precepts to them all, makes the Catholic position on reproductive technology crucial. This is magnified because the Catholic Church takes one of the more extreme positions on conception and contraception.

Over the last century, Catholic doctrine has held that there is an "inseparable connection" between the union of marriage and the procreative significance of sex. God established this connection, and humans may not break it. Catholic theologians believe that it is sinful to have sex in marriage while deliberately seeking to prevent procreation. Therefore, the Catholic Church forbids all artificial birth control methods because they change "natural" fertility. According to the catechism of the Catholic Church, the official compendium of church doctrine, "Fecundity is a good, a gift and an end [purpose] of marriage … Legitimate intentions on the part of the spouses do not justify recourse to morally unacceptable means (for example, direct sterilization or contraception)." Sex within marriage—the only acceptable context for sex according to church teaching—is tied very tightly to producing offspring.

In 1951, Pope Pius XII reaffirmed the Roman Catholic doctrine prohibiting the use of contraception. In recent years, however, statements made by Pope Francis have stirred uncertainty about whether church doctrine on contraception may change. In 2016, he was asked whether contraception or abortion was acceptable in areas affected by the Zika virus, which causes severe birth defects. While the pope condemned abortion, he offered a different perspective on contraception that many Catholics are still struggling to interpret. "[Pope] Paul VI, a great man, in a difficult situation in Africa, permitted nuns to use contraceptives in cases of rape," he said, adding that "avoiding pregnancy is not an absolute evil." Some have argued that Pope Francis was only talking about natural family planning, which involves abstinence. The church's official stance on contraception remains unchanged.

Catholic theologians believe that human life begins at the precise instant of fertilization. "From the time that the ovum is fertilized," wrote Cardinal Joseph Ratzinger (later Pope Benedict XVI), "a new life is begun which is neither that of the father nor of the mother; it is rather the life of a new human being with his own growth. It would never be made human if it were not human already." For Catholics, any form of abortion is murder, even "morning-after" birth control pills. "The human being is to be respected and treated as a person from the moment of conception," wrote the future pope, "and therefore from that same moment his rights as a person must be recognized, among which in the first place is the inviolable right of every innocent human being to life."

These positions create almost insuperable difficulties for Catholics who consider using IVF. "[I]n the usual practice of IVF, not all of the embryos are transferred to the woman's body; some are destroyed," wrote the future pope. "Just as the Church condemns induced abortion, so she also forbids acts against the life of these human beings." The Catholic Church also opposes any stem cell research that calls for the use of live embryos. "If the embryos are living, whether viable or not, they must be respected just like any other human person; experimentation on embryos which is not directly therapeutic is illicit."

This doctrinal rigidity reassures many believers but sometimes puts Roman Catholic couples around the world in an awkward position. The church generally extols the benefits children bring to their parents, their siblings, and society in general. Theologians encourage couples to have as many children as their circumstances make practical. Yet at the same time, the church forbids Roman Catholics from using artificial insemination, IVF, or other techniques to aid couples in creating the children they desire. The Roman Catholic Church states that physical sterility is not an absolute evil but a call from God to adopt children. Many Catholics do not consider this a satisfying response.

Even so, the majority of Catholic women in the United States have used contraception. A 2011 analysis by the Guttmacher Institute, a policy and research organization dedicated to reproductive health, found that 68 percent of American Catholic women who were sexually active but did not want to become pregnant were using contraception such as the birth control pill. What's more, 98 percent of Catholic women who had ever had sex had "used a method of contraception other than natural family planning." Many point to such statistics as evidence that the Catholic Church is not practically addressing the needs of Catholic women.

The Protestant Perspective

Protestants are Christians, but unlike Roman Catholics, they do not accept the authority of the pope. Rather, members of the Protestant denominations read and interpret the Bible in light of their own understanding. This has led to numerous Protestant sects, each with its own interpretations of religious and social issues.

Not surprisingly then, the Protestant response to reproductive technologies varies widely. There are about 800 million Protestants worldwide, including 170 million in North America. Moderate and liberal Protestant groups in the United States include

Defining "Natural" Procreation

When women reach their forties or fifties, they undergo menopause, a biological process in which they lose the ability to have a child. But IVF has allowed women to turn back their biological clocks and become pregnant in their fifties and even sixties. This is not a common occurrence; yet even after menopause, the uterus is fully capable of carrying out a pregnancy. In 1997, a sixty-three-year-old California woman, married for sixteen years without any children, had a healthy baby girl. Because of IVF, she became the oldest birth mother on record in the United States. Since then, more than a thousand women in their fifties and sixties have given birth in the United States.

For some people, the idea of technology assisting postmenopausal women to become pregnant presents no problem at all. They argue that age brings wisdom and maturity that can be as valuable in parenting as youth and energy. After all, many men become fathers in their late fifties or even when they're older.

However, opponents to this practice say it's "unnatural." The Roman Catholic Church often uses this line of reasoning by referring to natural law. "People have a basic, ethical intuition that certain behaviors are wrong because they are unnatural," writes one Catholic scholar. This thought can be extended by suggesting that if menopause sets a "natural" limit to pregnancy, it is not for humans to circumvent it. Just because people can do something, that doesn't mean they should do it.

However, an appeal to nature is not always a strong argument. Some things found in nature are not particularly beneficial (earthquakes, leukemia) or even morally acceptable (incest; parents killing their offspring). Some things that do not exist in the natural world (antibiotics, electric lights) have extremely desirable properties.

Episcopalians, Presbyterians, Methodists, and Lutherans. In general, these denominations today stress using the Bible to form a moral response to a situation, as opposed to the Roman Catholic emphasis on church doctrine as amplified by papal pronouncements. The Protestants have a variety of official responses to reproductive issues, but the liberal denominations generally support the right of individuals to make their own decisions regarding the use of reproductive technology.

Conservative Protestant groups include the Southern Baptist Convention, the Assemblies of God, and a variety of independent evangelical churches. These denominations insist on a more literal interpretation of the Bible than is used by other Protestants. They tend to take an uncompromising antiabortion position and so have often joined with Catholic allies to fight against stem cell research or any practice that would tamper with or discard embryos. In general, conservative, or fundamentalist, Protestants approve of the use of medicine and technology to correct physical problems that result in infertility, but they disapprove of reproductive methods that they feel violate the sanctity of marriage, such as the use of donated sperm and eggs.

The Jewish Perspective

In the Hebrew Bible, the commandment to have children is the first order given to Adam. Specifically, according to the biblical account, God told Adam to "be fruitful and multiply," and Jews have traditionally interpreted this as a commandment to fill the world with children.

Most Jewish scholars believe that this directive by God is so critical that it is permissible to accomplish it by natural or artificial means. Israel has more fertility clinics per capita than any other country and has among the world's highest per-capita rates of IVF procedures. The Israeli government will pay for up to six cycles of IVF treatments or the birth of up to two IVF children for any Israeli citizen. This is not because of unusually high infertility rates in Israel. Instead, it reflects the importance of reproduction in Judaism. Israel's relative permissiveness over the use of sperm and egg donation, surrogacy, and single and LGBTQ (lesbian, gay, bisexual, transgender, queer) parenthood stands in stark contrast to most of the Middle East.

Unlike Roman Catholics, Jews have no single religious leader authorized to proclaim definitive positions on complicated issues. However, most rabbinic authorities of all three major branches of Judaism (orthodox, conservative, and reform) agree that IVF and related techniques are acceptable for Jewish couples if the husband's sperm and the wife's eggs are used. However, many orthodox rabbis have not accepted the use of donor sperm—even though the practice is not technically considered adultery since sexual relations do not occur between the woman and the donor. Conservative and reform authorities are more open to allowing couples to use donor sperm for purposes of procreation.

Some rabbinical authorities reject outright the idea of using donor eggs. Others believe that a woman may receive donor eggs as long as her husband has consented. The question of "who is the mother" is critical in Orthodox Judaism because it affects the status of the baby. Traditional Jewish law determines a child's Jewish identity based on whether the mother is Jewish. If the genetic mother is not Jewish and the gestational mother is, what is the status of an infant born to the latter? The question is the subject of ongoing dispute in the orthodox community.

Jewish religious leaders have also debated the use of surrogacy and PGD. In general, infertile couples are allowed to secure the services of surrogates. PGD is acceptable to prevent the implantation of a fetus with genes for a heritable condition (such as Tay-Sachs disease), but unacceptable if used to select fetuses based on their sex. Jewish authorities believe the use of these

Demonstrators in Tel Aviv, Israel, in 2018 protest a new law that allows surrogacy for some but does not permit it for same-sex couples.

technologies for personal rather than medical reasons violates the commandment to "be fruitful and multiply."

All major Jewish denominations support stem cell research as long as it is for medical or therapeutic purposes. Traditional Judaism does not consider an embryo outside the womb to have the full status of a person. At the same time, Jewish tradition teaches that preserving life and promoting health are among the most precious of values. Therefore, stem cell research, which has the potential to save and heal human lives, has been deemed allowable.

Hinduism, Buddhism, and Other Religions

The major religions that originated in the Asian subcontinent of India, such as Hinduism, Buddhism, and Sikhism, all predate modern reproductive technologies. All three religions have sacred texts that are open to interpretation on the topic, and all lack a centralized authority to impose orthodox views on believers facing ethical dilemmas. The result is an extremely wide range of opinions.

Hinduism, the religion of an estimated one billion people in India and around the world, places great emphasis on fertility because of religious rituals and expectations that involve children. For instance, some rituals associated with securing one's afterlife must be performed by a son. Although dowries are now illegal in India, it is still widely expected that a son, upon marrying, will receive such a payment from the bride's family. A son is also expected to take care of his aging parents and to carry on the family name.

Abortion, condemned by traditional Hindu texts and teachings, has been legal in India since 1971; there were an estimated 6.4 million abortions in India in 2009. Nonmedical sex selection has become extremely controversial in India. The desire for sons and opposition to abortion place severe moral strains on some Hindu families who use modern reproductive technology.

In India, artificial insemination with the husband's sperm is acceptable. Because of popular Hindu ideas about biological descent, however, the use of donor sperm or eggs is not widely

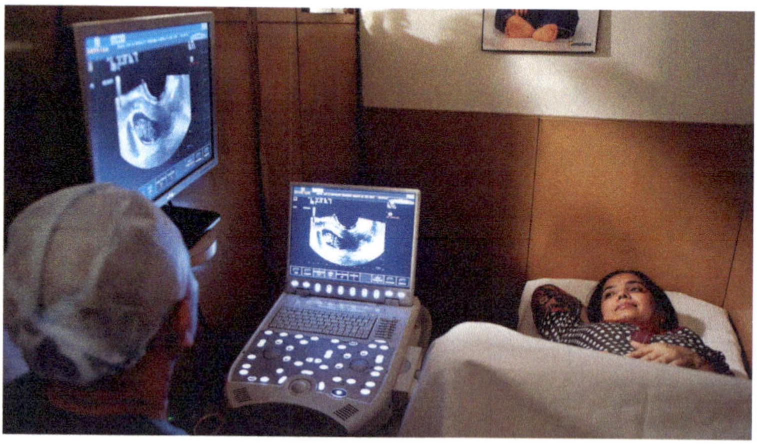

A doctor examines a woman in Mumbai, India, who may be serving as a surrogate mother. There is a large surrogacy industry in India.

practiced. Regarding IVF, many Hindu scholars suggest that all fertilized embryos must be implanted in order to avoid the destruction of any embryo. However, the nonhierarchical nature of Hinduism allows followers to form their own opinions.

In general, the various schools of Buddhism do not make definitive claims on right and wrong in the everyday activities of life. However, it is a basic Buddhist principle that a person should renounce worldly desires and pleasures. The desire to have a child so desperately that would-be parents would resort to IVF shows an attachment to the world that many Buddhists frown upon as an egocentric exercise in self-gratification.

Buddhists generally disapprove of abortion because of the belief in reincarnation. If individual human life begins at conception, the new being, bearing the karmic identity of a recently deceased person, is entitled to the same respect as any human being. A common Buddhist view is that preventing conception is ethically acceptable, while intervening after conception has occurred is not. For this reason, many Buddhists disapprove of IVF if it will result in the disposal of unneeded embryos. In the same way, many Buddhist scholars reject stem cell research, regardless of the researchers' good intentions, if spare embryos are destroyed.

However, disagreement is widespread on trickier reproductive technology issues. For example, traditional Buddhists may oppose abortion, but the procedure is extremely common in Buddhist South Korea despite its illegality. Estimates of the number of abortions performed annually in South Korea range from three hundred thousand to more than one million. This suggests that there is an unresolved difference of opinion between Buddhist teachings and practice regarding the moral status of embryonic life. "The society considers it a family issue," notes a Korean professor, "and there is a strong taboo against discussing a family matter in public."

Sikhism is, by some estimates, the fifth-largest religion in the world; as of 2010, about a half-million Sikhs lived in the United States. This relatively young faith (five hundred years old) has no explicit laws regarding fertility in its main sacred writings. Sikhs make their own personal choices on such matters. Still, many Sikhs believe that the creation of life is the will of God, and infertility is sometimes stigmatized in the Sikh community. Since God has given human beings the power of intellect, however, the use of reproductive technology is an acceptable way to achieve fertility. As in Hinduism and Buddhism, most Sikh religious leaders do not approve of any procedure that destroys or meddles with embryos. This can make IVF difficult to justify for traditional Sikhs.

Islam

There is no single perspective on reproductive technology among the approximately 1.8 billion Muslims of the world. In the 1980s, fatwas (legal rulings from recognized authorities) from scholars at Egypt's Al-Azhar University suggested that IVF and similar reproductive technologies were permissible if they did not involve any form of third-party donation of sperm or eggs. However, over the past two decades, Sunni Islam (the denomination of approximately 80 percent of Muslims) has become more conservative. Sunni religious leaders treat IVF with suspicion, although it may be permitted for a married couple if an artificially fertilized egg is replaced in the womb of the woman from whom the original egg was taken.

Sharia (Islamic law) places great emphasis on biological parentage. The Quran, the holy book of Islam, specifically reminds adoptive parents that they are not the child's biological parents. Adoption is prohibited in Islamic law and is actually illegal in

Egypt. For this reason, in the Sunni Muslim world, religious law prohibits both egg and sperm donation as solutions to infertility.

However, since the late 1990s, Muslims of the Shiite denomination have differed with their Sunni coreligionists over the acceptability of egg and sperm donation. As of 2010, Iran's leading ayatollah (authority on religious law) permitted gamete donation under certain conditions, and IVF is permitted, unlike in much of the rest of the Middle East. Shiites form the majority of Muslims in Iran, and this ruling has also had a significant effect in Lebanon, where a Shiite majority also seeks IVF services.

No matter their denomination, many Muslim men resist adoption and gamete donation with the argument that the resulting child won't really be theirs. However, some Muslims view the religious decrees as out of step with new developments in science and technology.

The Quran does not specifically mention abortion. This has resulted in differing viewpoints among Islamic theologians. Most early Islamic authorities permitted abortion within up to forty days (or less often, 120 days) of conception. However, laws in many Muslim nations are now written to reflect a more conservative interpretation of these rulings. Muslim legal scholars have generally made a clear distinction between the early stages of pregnancy (the first forty days) and the later stages. In general, Islamic scholars agree that the fetus acquires a soul at about four months, after which time the termination of a pregnancy is not permissible.

In regard to IVF and stem cell research, sharia usually draws a distinction between potential life (a fertilized egg in a dish) and actual life (a fertilized egg in a woman's womb). Most Muslim law sees the embryo as having the potential to grow into a human being but not yet qualifying to be called a human being. Therefore, Islam does not consider the destruction of embryos

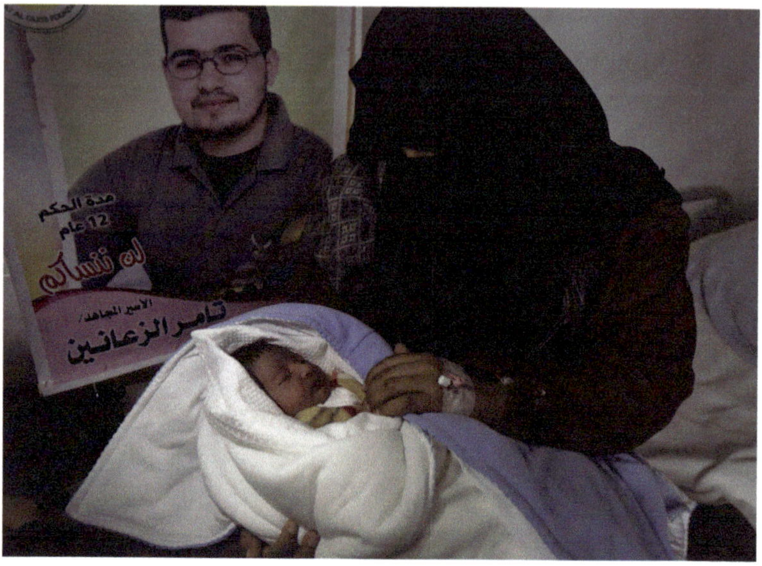

Palestinian mother Hanaa al-Zanen holds her newborn baby, conceived with her husband's sperm, which was smuggled out of an Israeli prison.

to be equivalent to infanticide. Muslim scholars believe that the embryo in this stage is not human because it is not in its natural environment and because it will not become a human being if doctors do not place it in a womb. Therefore, many Muslims support stem cell research, especially insofar as it has the potential to cure diseases. However, some conservative Muslim leaders now argue that the termination of an embryo at any stage of pregnancy is morally impermissible.

"Playing God"

Many forms of reproductive technology pose problems for adherents of religions that believe in a god (or many gods). By definition, gods are more powerful than humans. Religious traditionalists believe that the manipulation of genes and embryos is an attempt to control what ought to be an exclusively sacred process. Scholars from most religions worry that reproductive technologies may cause people to misunderstand their place in creation and to confuse humanity's role with that of a deity's. They believe that these techniques expose human beings to the temptation to go beyond the limits of a reasonable dominion over nature. For example, the Catholic Church condemns IVF as an act "that entrusts the life and identity of the embryo into the power of doctors and biologists and establishes the domination of technology over the origin and destiny of the human person."

"The problem lies in the hubris of the designing parents, in their drive to master the mystery of birth," writes one professor. This is a recurring complaint of religious theologians. Before assuming the papacy, Cardinal Ratzinger wrote that the researcher in reproductive technology "usurps the place of God ... [H]e sets himself up as the master of the destiny of others inasmuch as he arbitrarily chooses whom he will allow to live and whom he will send to death, and kills defenseless human beings."

Christianity, Judaism, and Islam point to the biblical account of the expulsion from the Garden of Eden in Genesis. The serpent tempts Eve, telling her that when she and Adam eat from the Tree of Knowledge, "your eyes will be opened and you will be like divine beings who know good and bad." The first couple ate from the tree, and God expelled them from Eden. A common interpretation of the story is that humans are tempted to be like God, but God will not permit people to be divine. When human beings try to assume divine powers, God will call them to account and exact a severe punishment.

Yet others point out that humans "play God" every time they use antibiotics, fly in an airplane, or text a friend. People tend to embrace technologies that control or harness nature because they think it improves the human condition. Whether reproductive technologies like IVF or PGD fit into this category is an open question.

Constitutional Freedoms

In the United States, the Roman Catholic Church owns and operates many hospitals and social service agencies. The opposition of the church to contraception, abortion, and IVF has sometimes put nonbelievers at risk of losing their jobs. For example, in the 1960s, Catholic hospitals sometimes expelled non-Catholic physicians for supporting birth control legislation or associating with Planned Parenthood.

The First Amendment to the US Constitution guarantees freedom of religion. However, this broad statement sometimes results in conflicts when an institution is seen as restricting individuals' ability to adhere to certain tenets of their religion. Roman Catholicism might classify homosexuality or IVF as sinful, but Catholic doctors and fertility specialists might not have the legal right to refuse to provide services for unmarried or same-sex couples, even if doing so would violate their religious beliefs. In general, religious groups do not have the right to apply religious criteria to activities outside their faith tradition.

Doctors in the United States are accustomed to choosing their own patients. As long as a person requesting treatment is not in a medical emergency, a physician is not obliged by law to treat him or her. However, a doctor's independence is not unlimited. No doctor or hospital receiving government funding, including money from Medicare and Medicaid, may discriminate against potential patients based on race, color, religion, or national origin. Many states have expanded these bans on discrimination to cover gender and sexual orientation.

In one case in California, a woman sued two doctors after one cited her personal "religious-based objections to treating homosexuals to help them conceive children by artificial insemination" and the other refused to authorize a refill of the patient's prescription for a fertility drug on the same grounds. In

North Coast Women's Care Medical Group v. Superior Court (2008), the California Supreme Court ruled that clinic doctors may not deny lesbians access to fertility treatment on the grounds that the procedure sought violates the physicians' religious beliefs. "The First Amendment's right to the free exercise of religion," wrote one judge, "does not exempt defendant physicians here from conforming their conduct to the … antidiscrimination requirements" of California's Civil Rights Act.

In 2009, the American Society for Reproductive Medicine (ASRM) issued a statement rejecting the restriction of access to fertility treatments based on a prospective parent's marital status or sexual orientation. They found no persuasive evidence that children are harmed or disadvantaged by being raised by single individuals, unmarried heterosexual couples, or gay and lesbian parents. Yet people who believe otherwise based on their religious traditions continue to oppose the ASRM position.

US law has not settled the question of whether doctors with religious objections to treating certain patients are exempt from these laws. However, in early 2018, the US Department of Health and Human Services announced it would create a Division of Conscience and Religious Freedom with the goal of defending medical professionals' right to refuse service based on their religious beliefs. The division was expected to permit health care workers to refuse to aid in abortions or help transgender individuals, among other scenarios.

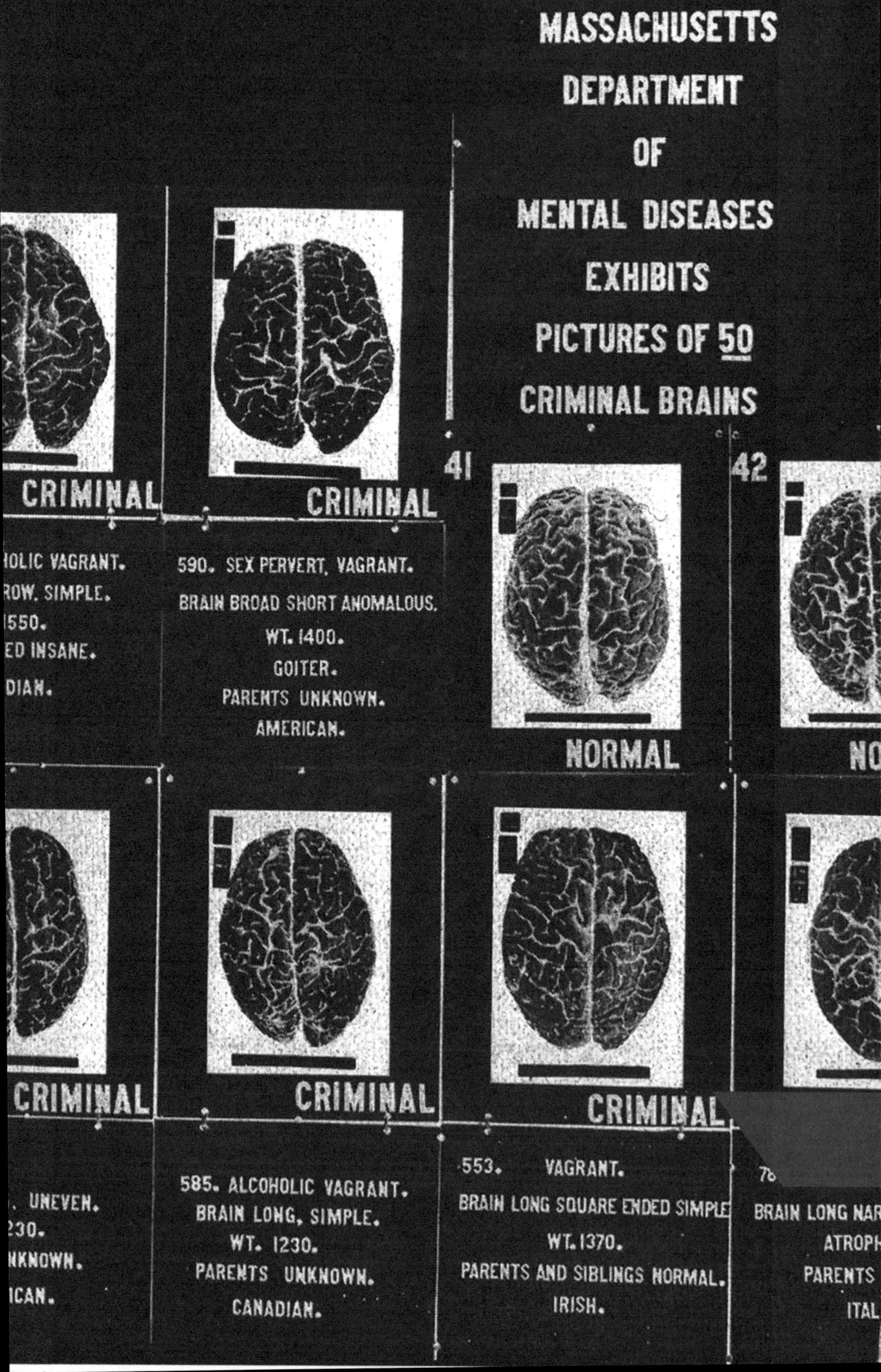
MASSACHUSETTS
DEPARTMENT
OF
MENTAL DISEASES
EXHIBITS
PICTURES OF 50
CRIMINAL BRAINS
CRIMINAL
CRIMINAL
41
NORMAL
42
590. SEX PERVERT, VAGRANT.
BRAIN BROAD SHORT ANOMALOUS.
WT. 1400.
GOITER.
PARENTS UNKNOWN.
AMERICAN.
CRIMINAL
CRIMINAL
CRIMINAL
585. ALCOHOLIC VAGRANT.
BRAIN LONG, SIMPLE.
WT. 1230.
PARENTS UNKNOWN.
CANADIAN.
553. VAGRANT.
BRAIN LONG SQUARE ENDED SIMPLE
WT. 1370.
PARENTS AND SIBLINGS NORMAL.
IRISH.

Chapter Three

THE TROUBLED HISTORY OF EUGENICS

Most proponents of the latest reproductive technologies still draw a line in certain cases. None of the questions surrounding the ethical application of these methods are drawn in black and white, and while some practices can be incredibly productive and helpful, those same practices in different contexts or used to different ends can be deeply troubling.

In the twenty-first century, supporters of genetic selection often tout it as a way to eliminate disease, produce healthier people, save money, and improve the world. While these arguments seem unquestionably positive, they must be approached with caution because the same claims were made in the name of eugenics in the early twentieth century, the most horrifying result of which was the Holocaust.

Opposite: A chart from the 1920s attempts to identify certain brain types with criminal behavior. Supporters of eugenics based their claims on such faulty science.

The first half of the twentieth century saw governments use laws, and sometimes violence, to interfere in reproductive decisions. These actions ranged from enforced sterilization to mass murder. The history of eugenics provides a warning about the dangers involved in the misuse of scientific advancement.

The Rise of Eugenics

The Englishman Francis Galton invented the word "eugenics" in 1883; he derived it from the Greek *eugenes*, meaning "wellborn." The word has since gained a negative connotation because of its regrettable history. In the first half of the twentieth century, however, people described eugenics as the science of the biological improvement of the human race.

Galton based his beliefs on the popularization, in the late 1800s, of Gregor Mendel's laws of heredity. Galton insisted that a wide variety of human physical, mental, and moral traits were inherited, and he concluded this meant that biology, not environment, shaped human culture. For thousands of years, humans had selectively bred desired characteristics into domestic animals and plants to weed out undesirable traits or weakness and promote the development of desirable characteristics. Galton believed that a eugenics movement could serve the same purpose for humans—to give "the more suitable races or strains of blood a better chance of prevailing speedily over the less suitable."

Galton's ideas about improving the human race grew in popularity after 1900 and gave rise to a worldwide movement. The popularity of eugenics was the result of a long process of intellectual and social change in the 1800s, in which people increasingly valued science and interpreted human life as the result of natural biological laws. The eugenics movement won many converts in Great Britain, the United States, Russia, Germany, and Latin America.

In some cases, the movement drifted from improving humans in general into an emphasis on preserving national and ethnic purity. In an era of rapid change, eugenics promised scientific control over evolutionary change, over social problems facing the middle and upper classes, and even over the future. It appealed to people who placed their faith in science as a way to solve human problems, and it was extremely popular with scientific, academic, and social elites in the first half of the 1900s.

The eugenicists promoted the idea that "human germplasm" was the most important thing in the world, the source of all human potential in a nation or race. Because of this, germplasm needed careful cultivation and conservation. Supporters of eugenics believed that the handicapped, the intellectually disabled, criminals, and the poor harmed the future of the human race by having too many children. They supported mental testing, extending birth control to poor people, restricting immigration, and sterilizing the "feebleminded" (a catch-all label used at the time to describe the intellectually disabled but also applied to promiscuous, poor, and uneducated women). According to eugenicists, the birthrate within these groups of so-called degenerates was skyrocketing because that population lacked intelligence and self-control.

In retrospect, the science of eugenics supported many troubling practices and claims. Defining which traits are the most desirable taps into subjective, culturally based assumptions and prejudices. The eugenic understanding of heredity incorporated blatant racism and class biases. Even at the time, opponents attacked the movement by observing that traits such as intelligence or character were impossible to define precisely and also were not controlled by one or a few genes.

Eugenicists also seemed to discount completely the role of environment in shaping individual human characteristics. A century of research has shown that mental disabilities are rarely hereditary and that the sterilization of the "feebleminded" would not significantly alter the prevalence of such disabilities in future generations. Even so, actions based on eugenics were to have tragic consequences for millions of people.

Forced Sterilization

In the United States of the 1920s and 1930s, eugenics was the centerpiece of a popular mainstream movement. Supporters advocated both positive and negative actions. Positive eugenics attempted to encourage marriage and a higher birthrate for people who were healthy and met the eugenicists' standards of intelligence and high moral character. The highly educated upper classes, who were beginning to have smaller families, were criticized for what Theodore Roosevelt called "race suicide."

Negative eugenics tried to discourage marriage and children among those its proponents characterized as "unfit," "feebleminded," or "diseased." Margaret Sanger, a pioneering feminist and birth control advocate, embraced eugenics. "More children from the fit, less from the unfit," she said, "that is the chief issue of birth control." Between the world wars, American eugenics took the political form of laws restricting immigration, encouraging the distribution of birth control to populations deemed by some to be less desirable, and the sterilization of criminals and the intellectually disabled.

In fact, the United States led the world in eugenics legislation. In 1907, Indiana passed the first law authorizing the compulsory sterilization of any "confirmed criminal, idiot, rapist, or imbecile" in a state institution whose condition had been determined "unimprovable" by an appointed panel of doctors. Supporters promoted the law as a cost-saving measure. If criminality and feeblemindedness were hereditary, involuntary sterilization would

Elaine Riddick was one of more than 7,600 people who were forcibly sterilized as part of North Carolina's eugenics program, 1929–1974.

not only save states large amounts of money, it would increase the genetic and economic efficiency of future generations.

By the late 1920s, two dozen states had passed involuntary sterilization laws that applied to the poor and sick inmates of mental institutions. By 1939, five more states had passed sterilization laws, and doctors had performed more than thirty thousand involuntary vasectomies (for males) and salpingectomies (for females). Some people opposed sterilization for its inhumane and undemocratic violation of an individual's rights, but they were in the minority. Most Americans saw sterilization as a beneficial and progressive policy. A poll by a national magazine in 1937 reported that 63 percent of Americans supported the compulsory sterilization of habitual criminals, while 66 percent endorsed the sterilization of the intellectually disabled.

The United States was not alone in supporting these policies. The same laws existed to a lesser degree in western Canada and in many European nations. The first eugenic sterilization laws in Europe were introduced in the canton of Vaud in Switzerland in 1928, and then in Denmark and Sweden. Between 1930 and 1949, more than eight thousand Danes and fifteen thousand Swedes were sterilized without their consent because they had been labeled sexually or mentally abnormal.

Eugenics in Nazi Germany

Eugenics turned out to be easily applied to other sinister projects. Adolf Hitler was a great admirer of America's eugenics legislation. "The demand that defective people be prevented from propagating equally defective offspring is a demand of the clearest reason," Hitler wrote in his autobiography, *Mein Kampf* (1926).

Germany passed the world's most extensive sterilization laws in 1933, almost as soon as Hitler and the National Socialists (Nazis) came to power. By the beginning of World War II in 1939,

Yugoslavian children who have been classified as "racially desirable" by the Nazis are moved to Austria in 1942, away from their parents.

special eugenics courts had ordered more than three hundred thousand Germans (about 1 percent of the population) to be sterilized—most for "congenital feeblemindedness," though nearly four thousand were sterilized for blindness and deafness. In the United States, many people supported the German program. One American eugenics expert complained, "the Germans are beating us at our own game."

The Nazis eventually translated eugenics into a program that attempted to maintain a "pure" German race under the banner of "racial hygiene." They tested their genetic theories by means of extensive studies involving live human beings. The work ranged from the measurement of physical characteristics to the sadistic

The Case of Carrie Buck

In 1924, Virginia adopted a sterilization law and then arranged a test case to win judicial approval. Carrie Buck (born 1906) was the unfortunate guinea pig. In the summer of 1923, she became pregnant after being raped by her adoptive mother's nephew. The family with whom she lived committed Carrie to an institution on the basis of results of an IQ test that gave her a mental age of nine (although her schoolwork was considered average). After the birth of Carrie's child, the superintendent recommended that the young woman be sterilized because she was "feebleminded" and a "moral delinquent."

In 1925, Buck's case went to the US Supreme Court. Lawyers for the state of Virginia argued that the state's police powers allowed its officers to make decisions for people like her. Buck's attorney, however, insisted that a state could not surgically deprive a person of his or her "full bodily integrity." If allowed to do so, he warned, "a reign of doctors will be inaugurated and in the name of science new classes will be added, even races may be brought within the scope of such regulation, and the worst forms of tyranny practiced." This would turn out to be an almost exact description of the racial purity program later undertaken in Nazi Germany.

The Supreme Court upheld the Virginia eugenics law in a nearly unanimous decision. Justice Oliver Wendell Holmes saw forced sterilization as a legitimate expression of a state's police powers. In delivering the court's ruling, Holmes concluded, "It is better for all the world, if instead of waiting to execute degenerate offspring for crime, or let them starve for their imbecility, society can prevent those who are manifestly unfit from continuing their kind."

A historic marker recalls the case of Carrie Buck, who was sterilized against her will under a Virginia eugenics law.

Buck was sterilized in October 1927, and other states passed laws similar to Virginia's. Buck's child, a daughter named Vivian, died at age eight in 1932. Modern research has revealed that, in fact, there was no "feeblemindedness" in the Buck family at all—Vivian also had an average record at school. Nonetheless, by the time the state legislature repealed the involuntary sterilization law in 1974, more than 7,500 people, including unwed mothers, prostitutes, and petty criminals, had undergone forced sterilization.

"experiments" carried out on twins in concentration camps. The German government also murdered tens of thousands of disabled people in institutions through compulsory "euthanasia" programs.

The Nazis murdered millions of European civilians, including Jews, Slavs, Gypsies, and homosexuals. The rhetoric and ideology of the eugenics movement helped make these mass killings acceptable to many scientists, physicians, geneticists, and members of the general population. The Nazis' brutal campaign, which resulted in the murder of six million Jews, was based on the belief that there were both "valuable" and "valueless" people in the world. The Nazis believed that Jews "valueless," and therefore disposable.

The Return of Eugenics

After World War II, there was widespread revulsion at the discovery of the Nazi atrocities committed in the name of eugenics. An almost universal backlash against such programs helped drive the concept underground. Eugenics was declared a pseudoscience—or a false science.

In the United States, however, many states maintained busy forced sterilization programs through the 1940s and 1950s.Thanks for the catch! Corrected. As recently as the mid-1960s, a few states were still sterilizing several hundred intellectually disabled people every year.

People were also being sterilized because of their race. By some estimations, between 25 and 50 percent of all Native American women were sterilized between 1970 and 1976. African American women received unnecessary hysterectomies—removing all or part of the uterus—in the South just to give medical students practice. And women of color were more likely to be targeted for sterilization on the grounds that it was better for society.

Only the emphasis on individual civil rights in the 1960s forced states to change their laws. Oregon repealed the last compulsory state sterilization law in 1983. In the early 2000s, the governors of Virginia, Oregon, California, North Carolina, and South Carolina made public apologies to the victims of their states' laws. Altogether, American doctors had sterilized about sixty thousand Americans without their consent.

However, if eugenics was temporarily out of style during and after the 1960s, it has reappeared since the creation of the world's first IVF baby in 1978. A few scientific researchers have openly called for the use of modern technology in promoting eugenic policies. According to one philosopher, "both justice and our obligations to prevent harm make genetic interventions to prevent disabilities not only permissible but also obligatory."

Distinguished scientists, including several Nobel laureates, have supported genetic screening that seems to border on eugenics. James Watson, the American biologist who helped discover DNA, said in 2003 that he backed genetic manipulation to make people more intelligent and better looking. "If you really are stupid, I would call that a disease," he said. "The lower 10 percent who really have difficulty, even in elementary school, what's the cause of it? A lot of people would like to say, 'Well, poverty, things like that.' It probably isn't. So I'd like to get rid of that, to help the lower 10 percent."

The lure of genetically manipulating children remains very strong. Some, however, argue that the new eugenics is not a movement of social reform to eliminate illness but mainly a way for privileged parents to have the kind of children they want and to increase their advantages in a competitive society. In 1993, for example, a poll revealed that 43 percent of Americans would use genetic engineering to enhance the physical appearance or intelligence of their child if that became a possibility.

Elsewhere in the world, governments continue to use regulation and intimidation to manipulate fertility. China began a mandatory one-child policy (with some exceptions) in 1980 in order to reduce the country's birthrate and increase per capita income. Parents who had more than one child faced large fines and could even lose their jobs. In the early years, enforcers carried out millions of sterilizations and abortions despite resistance in the countryside. China also enacted restrictions on marriages involving persons with certain disabilities or diseases. By 2010, China's fertility rate was an estimated 1.6 births per woman, one of the lowest rates in the world. In 1963, China's birthrate was about 44 births per thousand people; this had dropped to about 14 per thousand in 2009. In 2016, China adopted a two-child policy and that same year saw the highest number of births in seventeen years.

The twentieth-century history of eugenics casts a long shadow over today's debates about genetic engineering. Critics argue that human cloning and the quest for designer children are nothing more than "privatized" or capitalist eugenics. Defenders reply that genetic choices made freely are not eugenic in the negative sense that is now attached to the term.

"The core notion of eugenics, that people's lives will probably go better if they have genes conducive to health and other advantageous traits, has lost little of its appeal," writes a professor of philosophy and a supporter of the new eugenics. "Granted, when our society last undertook to improve our genes, the result was mayhem. The task for humanity now is ... to square the pursuit of genetic health and enhancement with the requirements of justice."

Whether this task can be accomplished is a central question in the debate over many reproductive technologies. "As we enlarge man's freedom, we diminish his constraints and that which he must accept as given," wrote an optimistic molecular biologist in the late 1960s. "We can be the agent of transition to a whole new pitch of evolution. This is a cosmic event."

The threat of twentieth-century eugenics casts a long shadow in both the scientific community and the public consciousness.

Modern debates around the ethics of genetic manipulation and preimplantation genetic diagnosis continue to look to these examples as a source of caution and guidance.

The Academy of Sciences of Hong Kong 港科院
SECOND INTERNATIONAL SUMMIT ON
HUMAN GENOME EDITING
Convened by
The Academy of Sciences of Hong Kong 港科院
THE ROYAL SOCIETY

Chapter Four

GENETIC ENGINEERING

In 2018, Chinese scientist He Jiankui claimed that he had edited the genes of newborn twin girls so that they were immune or resistant to human immunodeficiency virus, or HIV, a potentially deadly infection. Another baby whose genes had also been edited was still in the womb. Genome editing involves changing the complex set of traits or characteristics a child might inherit from a parent. Though his claims were unconfirmed, the announcement created an uproar across the globe. An investigation by the Chinese government found his claims were likely to be true.

Many argued that this was unethical, or that the ethical implications were unclear. Could such changes have unforeseen effects on the girls' health? On a broader scale, others worried that if such

Opposite: He Jiankui, a researcher from China, announced he had edited the genes of two newborn girls. A Chinese report claimed he had "seriously violated" state laws and faked an ethical review.

genome editing were to become widespread, it could take a sinister turn. As three science professors wrote in an op-ed in the *Washington Post* days after the news broke:

> *It's not hard to imagine features of human diversity that people might wish to modify in the name of giving their children a better life. In the United States, having dark skin correlates with higher risk of entanglement with law enforcement, with potentially dire lifetime consequences. Some parents might feel pressure to genetically alter the skin tone of their children. Far from fixing the social problems of an unequal world, this could well lead to new lines of discrimination between the genetically "perfected" and those left behind.*

Likewise, such editing could give a genetic advantage to those who can afford it, amplifying the divide between the rich and poor.

The eugenics movement of the early twentieth century attempted to control the breeding of human populations to improve the world's genetic fitness. Twenty-first-century geneticists look at this history and like to interpret it as a distant and irrelevant experience. However, reproductive technologies continue to involve issues of eugenics that present serious philosophical and moral challenges. The medical and moral implications are so complex that humanity is now considering major questions concerning how and even if genetic selection technologies will be used in the future.

Choosing Genes

Since the first in vitro fertilization (IVF) baby in 1978, other reproductive techniques have made it possible to choose particular genes or combinations of genes for one's child. The use of preimplantation genetic diagnosis (PGD) allows people to select embryos of a particular sex and to screen for nonmedical traits, such as height and eye color. As reproductive technologies develop, many people are concerned that a child may be turned into a consumer item whose main purpose is to satisfy the emotional needs of parents, leading many to call such genetically selected children "designer babies."

There seems to be little doubt that such techniques will become even more precise in the near future, which raises even more questions. What kind of genetic selection should be permissible at the embryo stage? Is it ethical to avoid intellectual or other disabilities in potential children? Should people be allowed to select for the possibility of greater intelligence? Should it be legal to choose to have a child only of a particular sex?

Genetic analysis also allows parents to create children through IVF whose genes can help others. For example, parents can choose to have a genetically matched child who is able to donate life-saving tissue to a sick sibling suffering from Fanconi anemia and in need of a donor. However, some people question whether a child should be brought into the world simply for the sake of serving as a donor to another person.

Choosing Sex

The development of ultrasonography and amniocentesis in the mid-1970s allowed parents to learn the gender of their child before birth, and the decriminalization of abortion afforded choices about continuation or termination of pregnancy for reasons including fetal sex. More recently, PGD has allowed people who use IVF to choose the preferred sex of their baby at the embryo stage, and further advances in reproductive technologies, such as improved techniques of sperm sorting, can virtually ensure the sex of a future child.

Sometimes, parents choose the sex of a child for medical reasons. They might choose a female fetus to rule out X-chromosome-linked conditions such as Duchenne muscular dystrophy and hemophilia if there is a family history of one or more of these conditions. There is virtually no ethical debate over this choice.

However, sex selection sometimes occurs for nonmedical reasons. Some parents have used prenatal testing to balance the number of boys and girls in the family. Other parents may simply prefer one sex to the other. Sex selection for nonmedical reasons has become one of the most controversial issues related to modern reproductive technologies.

In some Asian countries, the preference for sons is driving many families to abort female fetuses. According to one estimate, ninety million women were "missing" from census totals in 2005 from Afghanistan, Bangladesh, China, India, Pakistan, South Korea, and Taiwan, possibly as a result of sex-selective abortion. This practice, known as female feticide, appears to be cultural rather than economic. Large differences in sex ratios do not seem to exist in sub-Saharan Africa, Latin America, or the Caribbean.

In India, longstanding cultural traditions favor a son over a daughter. According to one controversial study, parents in northwestern India were estimated to abort a half-million female fetuses each year. When the first ultrasound clinic opened in the state of Punjab in 1979, there were 925 girls for every 1,000 boys younger than seven; by 1991, the number of girls was 875, and by 2001, it had dropped to 793. It is estimated that, between 1980 and 2010, four to twelve million female fetuses were aborted in India because of their sex.

New technology drives some of these changes. Many families in Asia (and around the world) have easy access to ultrasound scans

Indian prime minister Narendra Modi celebrates International Women's Day in 2018.

for determining the sex of an unborn child, as well as inexpensive abortions for parents who do not want a female baby. "Vietnamese women who find they are carrying an unwanted female baby often head immediately to an abortion clinic," reported one Singapore newspaper. "A walk-in abortion at a state hospital can be performed for $10 and at private clinics for about $20."

In the United States, about eight states have banned sex-selective abortions. There is some evidence that abortions regularly take place for this reason in the United States, although in past polls, most Americans have expressed their opposition to it.

Prenatal sex selection presents a number of ethical dilemmas. One objection draws on an argument familiar from the abortion debate. If embryos are people, then discarding unused embryos in the course of IVF—no matter the reason—is the same as murder.

The main argument against nonmedical sex selection is that it devalues one sex—usually the female—and reinforces discrimination. Sex selection for nonmedical reasons often favors the birth of sons. "You don't have to be a feminist to know that being a girl is not a birth defect," says one analyst.

The effects of feticide may ultimately have societal implications. It is hard to predict the future of societies with vastly unbalanced gender ratios. However, it is possible that countries with many more young men than women will run into problems. There are an estimated 33.6 million more men than women in China—and the gap may be even wider than that—and as a result, it's become difficult for many men—especially those from poorer or more rural backgrounds—to get married.

Some people believe that sex-selective abortion following prenatal sex testing is so obviously discriminatory that they have called on governments to condemn and restrict the practice. The Council of Europe's Convention on Human Rights and Biomedicine states, "The use of techniques of medically assisted procreation shall not be allowed for the purpose of choosing a future child's sex, except where serious hereditary sex-related disease is to be avoided."

National governments have taken a variety of stances. Canada's Assisted Human Reproduction Act prohibits sex selection in reproductive technology (except for a sex-linked disorder). The Indian government has made it a crime to abort a fetus because of gender and has outlawed the use of ultrasound machines to reveal whether a woman is carrying a boy or a girl. In some places, the change has been dramatic. A crackdown in the Panipat district—along with the Beti Bachao Beti Padhao ("Save a Girl, Educate a Girl") campaign—resulted in an increase from 822 girls born per 1,000 boys in 2011 to 945 girls per 1,000 boys in 2017. This crackdown has involved raids on illegal medical centers where parents learn the sex of their fetuses via ultrasound.

On the other hand, the United States remains one of the few countries that mostly permits nonmedical sex-selective abortion. One survey of the American fertility industry showed that, of the clinics offering embryo screening with IVF, 80 percent would do nonmedical sex selection of embryos if prospective parents requested it.

Even though females bear the brunt of nonmedical sex selection, restricting the practice would interfere with reproductive rights that women have struggled to achieve for centuries. Many feminists believe that women must gain full control over their own reproductive lives if they are to free themselves from male control. Therefore, they resist any attempts to declare rules for determining when an abortion is justified as a limitation on female choice.

Yet not all sex selection is discriminatory. Parents in North America and Europe often perform nonmedical sex selection for the sake of balancing families. Opponents argue that there is nothing inherently wrong with "unbalanced" families. However, couples with two boys might want a girl, and vice versa. Some argue that to assume that all gender choices are sexist is unfair.

"Mothers who want boys should have boys and mothers who want girls should have girls," writes one bioethicist. "Pre-implanting diagnosis offers the promise of increasing the number of children who are loved and wanted ... [O]nce one crosses the threshold of believing that abortions should be available on demand, because women ought to control their own bodies and all pregnancies should be wanted, then investigating the motivations of individuals seeking abortions makes little sense."

"Designer Babies"

Some people fear that sex selection is a slippery slope and may lead to parents arranging for "designer babies." It is not clear whether parents will ever be able to select for children's intelligence or athletic ability—an undertaking that would probably involve many genes and could not exclude environmental factors that lead to success in these areas. However, in the twenty-first century, scientists will most likely develop the capability for some gene selection—and, as one commentator puts it, "Selection is the first step to design."

In the United States, decisions regarding PGD are currently in the hands of doctors or clinics. The ASRM makes suggestions, but these voluntary guidelines in a profit-driven industry are not always followed. In fact, most of the American fertility industry, an enterprise valued at more than $4.5 billion per year, is unregulated. It is limited only by the current state of science and technology, the desires of clients, their ability to pay, and the availability of a clinic willing to follow their wishes. Many worry that such a situation leaves the door open to designing children.

Not everyone fears this future. Some parents buy their children advantages by enrolling them in expensive schools, providing them with swimming lessons and SAT preparation courses, and so on. No one thinks less of these parents; in fact, most people admire them for trying to do the best for their children. Supporters of "designer children" argue that selecting traits in a fetus is not fundamentally different from postnatal methods of performance enhancement. If the technology exists to help children, people should be allowed to use it.

"I don't think testing for freckles or blond hair or musical aptitude is a morally bad thing to do," said the director of the Center for Bioethics. "I think parents will want to do it, so I think it will expand rapidly." In fact, according to one commentator, parents are "morally obligated to genetically modify their children" if possible. Parents should use technology to manipulate their children's "memory, temperament, patience, empathy, sense of humor, optimism" in order to give them "the best opportunity of the best life."

American society permits almost unlimited reproductive freedom—whether or not to have children at all, when to have them, with whom to have them, and how many children to have. Given these freedoms, it seems logical that prospective parents should also be able to choose some of their children's characteristics. Most people support freedom of choice as long as they are not causing serious harm to their children or others. They do not want the government intruding by asking about their motives for having children.

One mother of twins from donated eggs gave a good synopsis of the argument for choosing the genetic traits of one's children. When picking an egg donor, "I basically picked me, but younger and prettier," she said. "We read the same books, we both ran marathons, we had the same outlook on life." She said that handpicking the best donor is really just about giving your kids the best start: "If this person is an Ivy-educated person and they have really great genes, why wouldn't you want to do that for your kids?"

Others, though, are horrified by the idea of genetic selection. Some scientists have claimed to have the ability to seize control of evolution through conscious design. These statements seem to echo the goals of twentieth-century eugenics, in which scientists viewed people as products to be managed and improved. Bioengineering breakthroughs in the fields of muscle enhancement, memory enhancement, height enhancement, and sex selection all began as an attempt to treat a disease or prevent a genetic disorder. However, they quickly moved out of the medical realm as people began suggesting their use for personal applications. What began as a medical solution drifted into the marketplace as a consumer choice for those wealthy enough to afford it.

Some would also argue that genetic engineering is wrong because it violates a child's right to autonomy. A genetically designed child is indebted and subordinate to the designing parent in a way that a child born from an unplanned beginning is not. "Designed" children are not fully free because even favorable enhancements, such as for musical talent, would point children toward particular life choices, whether the child supports those choices or not.

Supporters of genetic enhancement reject this argument. The alternative to genetic enhancement is a child who is at the mercy of the genetic lottery, they say. Those who favor genetic enhancement question why a random distribution of talents is

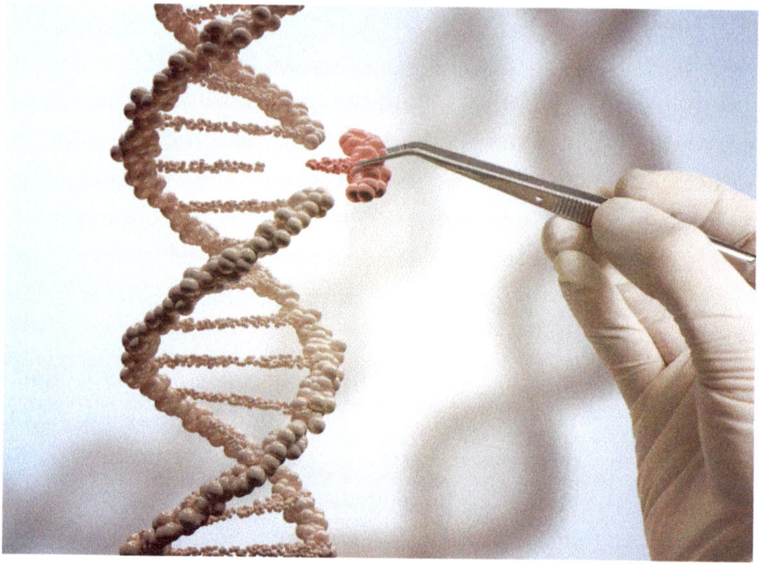

Some argue that genetic editing can not only pose a danger to the child but raises socioeconomic concerns about access to such technologies.

better than a world in which the same talents are consciously given to children in advance.

Another argument against "designer babies" points out that it is impossible to predict the ultimate outcome of manipulating natural selection and the genetic makeup of humankind. Trait selection may result in benefits, but it may also trigger the law of unintended consequences, leading to horrendous outcomes that science cannot predict.

Opponents of genetic selection also point to its potential for echoing the eugenics of the twentieth century in another way: such selection might favor or disfavor certain racial characteristics, for example. Also, because it will most likely be an expensive procedure, it might only be accessible to the wealthy, broadening the divide between rich and poor as the children of the wealthy gain even more advantages—this time, genetic ones—over those of the poor and middle class.

The Debate over Desirable Genes

Genetic tests for disabilities are increasingly allowing people with a family history of genetic disease to select healthy offspring. However, some might wish to select for a trait that others consider a disability. One study found that 3 percent of American clinics surveyed had used genetic screening to enable parents to select an embryo "for the presence of a particular disease or disability ... in order that the child would share that characteristic with the parents." Is this a legitimate expression of human freedom or a perversion of it? And who can be the judge of such requests?

In 2001, Sharon Duchesneau and Candy McCullough, a deaf couple in the United States, were looking for a sperm donor who was congenitally deaf. A series of sperm banks rejected the couple, so they instead used a sperm donor of their own selection. A deaf friend with five generations of deafness in his family contributed the sperm that was used to impregnate Sharon Duchesneau. A boy, Gauvin, was born on Thanksgiving Day 2001 with limited hearing.

Because Duchesneau and McCullough had used a private donor, Duchesneau had the right to procreate with whomever she and McCullough might choose. Like many people in the deaf community, these parents did not see deafness as a medical condition that needed repair. Instead, they viewed it as an established cultural identity with a basis in American Sign Language. While she was pregnant, Duchesneau explained, "It would be nice to have a deaf child who is the same as us. I think that would be a wonderful experience ... A hearing baby would be a blessing. A deaf baby would be a special blessing."

Other deaf couples have used prenatal genetic testing of their fetus to select a deaf child. They argue that their choice is no different from choosing a child's sex. A spokesperson for the British Deaf Association made this point: "The real issue is not whether people are trying to design deaf babies, but how society currently denies deaf children to enjoy the same rights, responsibilities, opportunities, and quality of life as everyone." Duchesneau and McCullough wrote, "being deaf is a positive thing, with many wonderful aspects."

The choice to create a child with special challenges is not unique to the deaf population. Little people may wish to have a child who is a little person. People with a cognitive disability may wish to have a child like them. Mixed-race couples may wish to choose the skin color of their child. Commenting on the selection made by Duchesneau and McCullough, one doctor said, "This is an inevitable result of deciding that we allow people to have a choice over what sort of child they are going to produce."

However, the decision to choose a deaf child attracted fierce criticism. Many people regard the couple's desire as profoundly selfish, the worst possible example of "designer babies." "This is another example of reproductive technology running riot," one researcher complained. "To deprive a baby of a natural faculty is unethical behavior." He argued that deaf people are denied the world of sound, music, and the most fundamental form of human communication.

Yet, even assuming for the sake of argument that choosing to bring a hearing-impaired child into the world is unethical, does that make it illegal? In the United Kingdom, the answer is yes. As of 2018, the British government's Human Fertilisation and Embryology Authority Code of Ethics read:

> *Embryos that are known to have a gene, chromosome or mitochondrion abnormality involving a significant risk that a person with the abnormality will have or develop:*

a. a serious physical or mental disability
b. a serious illness, or
c. any other serious medical condition, must not be preferred to those that are not known to have such an abnormality.

A deaf British couple who wanted a deaf child objected to the law. They did not believe the state should be able to dictate to people which of their embryos they could select and which they could reject. The law meant that the government could compel the couple to discard the very embryos that they wanted to implant. One of them said, "I couldn't participate in any procedure which forced me to reject a deaf embryo in favour of a hearing embryo."

Prenatal Genetic Testing

The number of prenatal genetic tests available has increased quickly, having jumped from about 100 in 1993 to 1,000 in 2003. Many prospective parents use such technology to detect major fetal health problems before birth. More controversially, some may end the pregnancy if prenatal testing reveals a disability or a serious at-risk condition. There is no known chemical or surgical remedy if a child-to-be has cystic fibrosis, fragile X syndrome, Down syndrome, Tay-Sachs disease, or anencephaly.

However, people at risk of producing a child with an incurable condition may be reluctant to terminate a pregnancy. They may even refuse genetic testing to avoid finding themselves in such a position.

Is it morally acceptable to abort a fetus likely or certain to be deaf or blind? How intellectually or developmentally disabled must a fetus be before abortion is justifiable or ethical? What if the child is at risk of developing a serious disease, such as

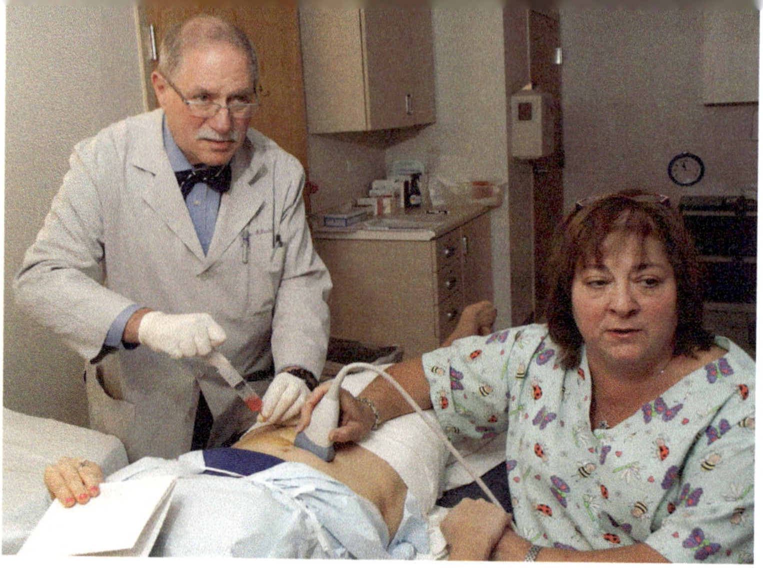

Dr. Norman Ginsberg (*left*) works with sonographer Sandra Concialvi (*right*) to extract a patient's placental tissue for genetic testing.

Huntington's, later in life? To what degree do parents, doctors, and society have the right to choose which babies come into the world? There are no regulations to guide parents and doctors in making ethical decisions about whether to terminate or go forward with particular pregnancies.

As a result, some doctors fear that prenatal science is drifting into eugenics. A 1995 survey of American genetics professionals found that about 30 percent would abort a pregnancy if the child were destined to be severely obese. Doctors have reported couples terminating pregnancies for poor vision or an extra finger.

An argument can be made for retaining even embryos destined to have severe disease. "Most people with disabilities rate their quality of life as much higher than other people think," said a director of the World Institute on Disability. "People make the decision [to reject embryos] based on a prejudice that having a disability means having a low quality of life." A man, citing as an example his cousin Suzie, an adult with Down syndrome, said, "There's a lot of kids born into the world that have severe problems and that doesn't stop them from having a life or having a lot of love to give. If my aunt and uncle would have terminated that pregnancy we would never have known Suzie."

Others point out that, because people with Down syndrome generally suffer from cognitive impairment and health problems, many are never able to live independently or achieve financial security. This tasks families with the lifelong work of taking care of that child, which can be quite expensive and labor-intensive. "Down syndrome is life-altering for the entire family," writes Ruth Marcus in the *Washington Post*.

The experience of a woman who used modern reproductive technology encapsulates the dilemma. Having had two brothers who died in their early twenties from muscular dystrophy, the woman was hoping to avoid having a child who possessed the genes for the disease. "If this technology was there, would my brothers ever have been born?" she asks. "It becomes: Did their lives have value? Absolutely, they had value. But it was also tragic to see how young they died."

At one time, giving birth to a child with Down syndrome was a matter of chance. Today, an area once governed by fate now offers an element of choice. Many parents of children with Down syndrome or another congenital disability report feeling judged or blamed for having their children. It is true that prospective parents are free to choose whether to act on the results of prenatal testing. However, they are not free to escape the burden of choice that the new technology creates. Doctors now estimate that more than two-thirds of women who get positive test results for Down syndrome choose abortion.

On the other hand, it seems a plain fact that a healthy newborn is surely the best outcome for any pregnancy. In the end, genetic tests allow future parents to select the child—from the possible children they could have—with the best opportunity of having the best life. For that reason, doctors offer prenatal testing for

The Rights of the Unborn

Parents might want a deaf child, but what about what the child wants? A central question is where to draw the dividing line between society's interest in protecting the unborn versus parental freedom to choose. The consent of an unborn child obviously cannot be obtained, but do unborn children possess any rights—even before conception?

Derek Parfit (1942–2017) was a British philosopher specializing in problems of personal identity and ethics. He argued that as long as a resulting child will have a "life worth living," the child cannot be harmed by an act that brought about his or her existence. This is because even an impoverished life is better than not existing at all. In discussing these circumstances, philosophers use the term "nonidentity problem."

If this reasoning is correct, then Gauvin, the deaf child, has no complaint. If his mothers had not selected a deaf donor, he would never have existed at all. Surely it is better for him to be alive than to have never been born. Although there is obviously a subjective component to deciding whether any disease or flaw is sufficiently severe to make life *not* worth living, almost no one would say that deafness is that severe.

The nonidentity problem seems to imply that the reproductive choices of parents can almost never harm a future child and therefore should not be restricted by law. Only the decision to create a child whose life, because of medical ailments, would be worse than not existing at all would constitute harm. In these rare cases, the law could restrict parents from creating a child with a severe genetic disability.

Courts have usually rejected wrongful-life lawsuits in which disabled people sue doctors for the suffering they incur by being alive. These arguments essentially insist that the person is "better off dead," and courts have ruled that it is impossible to weigh any suffering versus nonexistence.

Down syndrome, hemophilia, cystic fibrosis, and other genetic conditions. The effects of these diseases are generally negative, and societies everywhere seek to reduce their impact. No reasonable person would choose sickness over health. If people have the ability to choose, why not choose health?

"Savior Siblings"

Adam Nash was born in 2000 with the specific task of helping to rescue Molly, his older sister. Molly Nash had Fanconi anemia, a rare genetic disease. Molly would die unless her parents could produce a perfectly matched donor for a bone marrow stem cell transplantation. The Nashes created thirty embryos and went through four cycles of IVF to produce Adam, who was the exact match Molly needed. In the end, the process worked perfectly. "She's a typical teenage girl, she loves to dance, loves the theater," said Molly's mother in 2010. "We never thought she would live to see 15."

Adam was the first "savior sibling" born in the United States. "Savior sibling" refers to the creation of a genetically matched human being who is able to donate life-saving tissue to a sick sibling in need of a donor. The process of creating savior siblings requires the creation of embryos by IVF. Then the embryos are tested by means of PGD, and doctors implant the one that is genetically compatible into the mother's womb. When that baby is born, doctors collect the umbilical cord blood—a rich source of stem cells. Stem cells can produce many types of blood cells and can treat and even cure several different blood disorders. Such stem cells can produce bone marrow, blood, or even organs that are a perfect match for the sick sibling. Several high-profile cases of savior siblings in the United States, Great Britain, and Australia have sparked a range of reactions.

Many people feel the decision to allow the creation of savior siblings is a triumph of common sense, especially since prohibition of this use of technology would result in the suffering and preventable deaths of existing children who could have been saved by sibling donation. "People are certainly entitled to their opinions," says Molly Nash's mother, "but we were doing what was best for our family." Because a ban on the use of PGD to create savior siblings would be fatal for some children, supporters argue that the burden of proof rests with people who are opposed to the concept.

Many opponents argue that the ultimate consequences of savior siblings are worse than the deaths of a certain, likely limited, number of children. They see creating savior siblings as a form of selective breeding and so, to them, the connection to twentieth-century eugenics is too close for comfort. If doctors created thirty embryos before parents selected one, it is possible to say that the ultimate "winner" was born only because of "good" genes, while other embryos were not chosen because they had the wrong genetic makeup. Savior siblings seem to many like an enticing step down the dangerous slippery slope to screening for looks and intelligence.

A second claim echoes the argument against "designer" children—that a savior sibling is a commodity, a means rather than an end. Parents are creating children based on the parents' own needs and desires.

Yet it is also true that all parents have a variety of reasons for starting a family, and many of these reasons may not be in the interest of the future child. Some parents want a basketball star. Others need children to work in the fields or to take care of them when they get old. Still others have children by accident. Are these reasons inherently more ethical than the idea of a savior sibling?

Some bioethicists worry that children born from such procedures would feel unloved. They might see themselves as exploited and not wanted for themselves, but only for being the means to save the life of a sibling. Would a child conceived for this reason be more or less likely to enjoy a loving relationship with his or her parents or siblings? Given the novelty of the

When Adam Nash was born, his umbilical cord blood was able to help his sister, Molly (*left*), recover from Fanconi anemia.

concept, there is no empirical evidence of whether savior siblings are happier or less happy than other children.

These arguments deal mainly with the donation and use of umbilical cord tissue, as opposed to nonrenewable solid organs (such as kidneys). In donations of the latter type, a savior sibling risks real physical harm. Such a situation was fictionalized in *My Sister's Keeper*, Jodi Picoult's best-selling novel, which was adapted into a movie in 2009. It is possible, some argue, that the use of umbilical cord tissue might lead down the slippery slope to organ transplants.

It is extremely tricky to balance the life and medical needs of an existing child, the rights of a future sibling, and the reproductive freedom of parents. In Great Britain, the Ethics Committee of the Human Fertilisation and Embryology Authority recommended in 2001 that PGD be allowed for the creation of savior siblings. However, the next year, the committee reversed these recommendations because of concern about the psychological burden placed on the future child. In 2004, the body again changed policy based on improved PGD techniques.

Today, the creation of savior siblings is permitted in certain instances in the United Kingdom. There is no federal regulation regarding this issue in the United States.

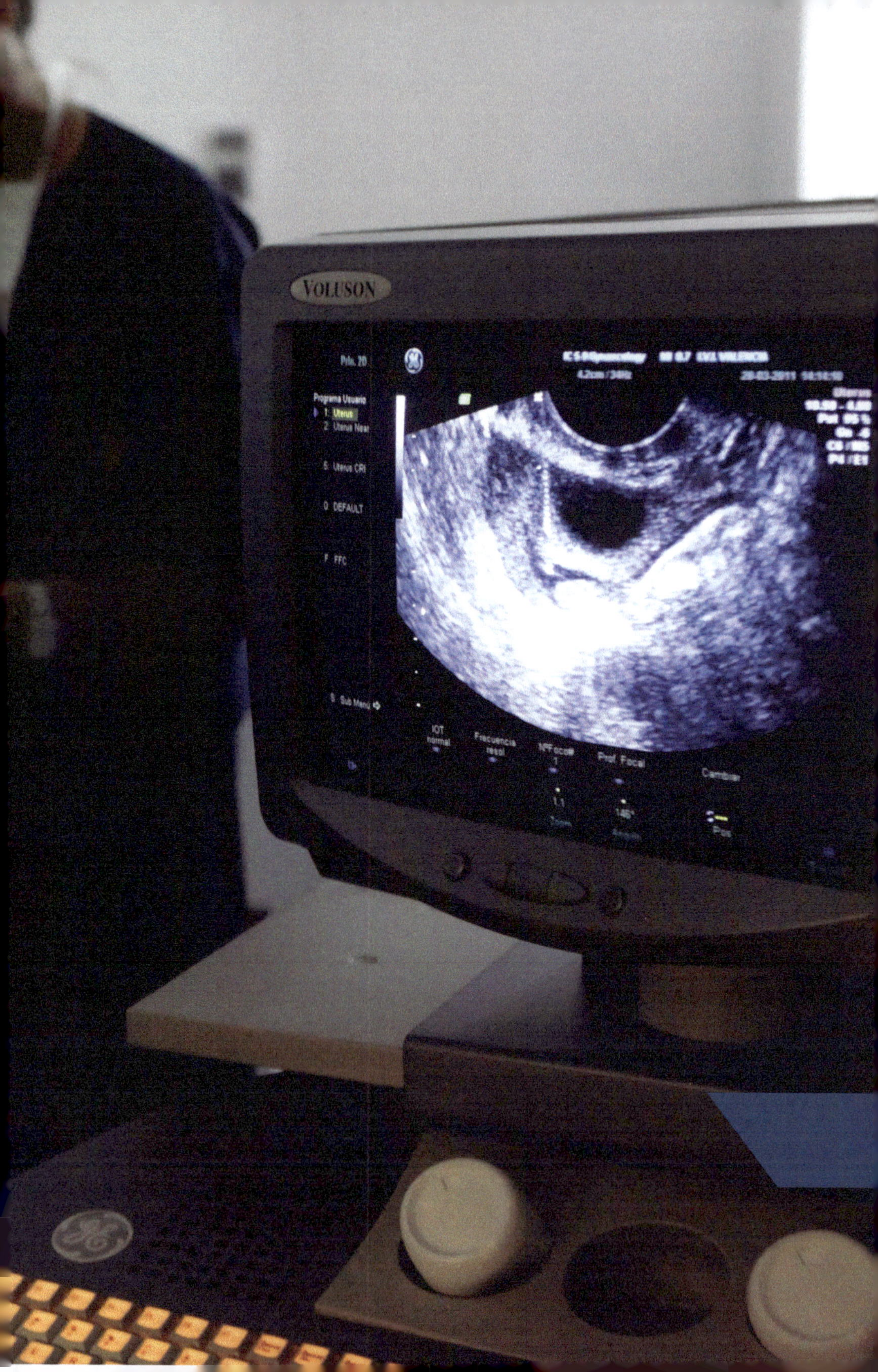
VOLUSON
Programa Usuario
1: Uterus
0 DEFAULT
F FFC
IOT
normal
Frecuencia
resol
Prof. Focal
Cambiar

Chapter Five

DONATING EGGS AND SPERM

The donation of sperm and eggs has led to the birth of millions of babies over the years. Many celebrate this, pointing out how many families were started thanks to these donations. At the same time, a variety of ethical dilemmas have surrounded the practice. This has been compounded by the growing ease of access to DNA tests, which have helped many children produced through such donations find their genetic half-siblings and go in search of their donor parents.

Paying Donors

Egg donation is restricted in many countries; for example, it is illegal to buy eggs directly from a donor in Canada. In 2019 in the United States,

Opposite: An ultrasound machine is used during a medical procedure in which a woman in Valencia, Spain, donates her eggs.

however, paying for eggs remains legal. Nearly 21,200 pregnancies with donor eggs were attempted in 2015, up from 1,800 in 1992.

When women donate eggs, they often experience serious side effects. Doctors first use strong medication to cause the release of excess eggs, then insert a needle through the abdomen to harvest the eggs. Egg donation can cause abdominal swelling, mood swings, and hot flashes. Donors may also risk future fertility problems. Critics say they fear that young women may not understand the potential physical and psychological risks, including how they might feel years later about the experience.

At first, most donated eggs came from a recipient's friends or family. However, demand for human eggs grew because of advances in infertility treatments and increased investment in stem cell research. Young women at prestigious colleges are now recruited to donate their eggs through advertising in student newspapers, on websites such as Facebook and craigslist, and even on highway billboards. Glamorous potential donors have asked for as much as $100,000.

Clinics and brokers generally tell women to donate no more than six times. However, adherence to the guidelines is voluntary. There is nothing to prevent a woman from exceeding the limit. Demand for donors is keen, and the money is good. One woman said, "It seemed a relatively small amount of my time for what seemed to be pretty decent compensation." To which a scornful doctor replied, "This is not a career path."

Payment for egg and sperm is the source of much debate. The American Society of Reproductive Medicine (ASRM), the professional association that oversees the field, suggests that payments of more than $5,000 beyond medical and related expenses "require justification" and that payments above $10,000 "are not appropriate." The guidelines also recommend that women not receive more money based on their looks or intelligence. However, the ASRM guidelines are not binding. In fact, as of 2010, there were almost no laws, rules, or regulations governing egg donation in the United States. Virtually anyone can open for business as an "egg donor agency" and recruit young women as donors.

One study examined more than one hundred egg donation ads from sixty-three college newspapers and found that one-quarter offered compensation exceeding the $10,000 ASRM guidelines. About the same proportion of ads required a minimum SAT score, and most contained appearance or ethnicity qualifications. Some ads offered to pay more for women who were tall, blonde, or thin. Every hundred-point difference in a university's average SAT scores correlated to an increase of more than $2,000 in the fees advertised for potential egg donors. Some ads at elite colleges promised $35,000 for donors. Critics argued that donors were seduced by payments to do something that they might later regret. One doctor commented, "They'll look at the money on offer and will overlook some of the risks."

In 2009 in California, a state that had already banned the sale of eggs for research purposes, the legislature passed a law requiring that egg donor advertisements include specific warnings about health risks. At the same time, though, New York's Empire State Stem Cell Board decided that the state could pay women up to $10,000 for donating eggs for research.

Those who support payment argue that an egg donor will experience physical consequences and may undergo great emotional and social stress. Therefore, she should be paid for what she has gone through. Supposedly, the payment is actually for effort, not for eggs. An ASRM spokesperson complained that concerns expressed about egg donation bordered on gender discrimination. "It's interesting to me that people get upset about egg donation in ways they don't get upset about sperm donation," he said. "You never hear discussions about, 'Oh, the sperm donor is going to regret it someday that they have a child.'"

In fact, some sperm donors do express regret. One father says he spends "considerable time these days fretting about possible extra offspring … [and] worries that children he helped create are out there looking for him, tortured by the fog that blurs their beginnings, when he could make them feel better."

In the United States, most sperm donors who donate through a sperm bank receive some kind of payment. Payment for a sperm sample is usually less than $150, an amount so low that the incentive to donate is not considered to be coercive for the donor. Still, when Canada's reproductive technology law in 2004 made it illegal to buy sperm or eggs, the end of the $75 payment to donors may have led to the shortage of sperm in Canada.

The United States, on the other hand, had an increase in sperm donors during the economic recession of the late 2000s. "If they're willing to go through the process it can be worth it in the end," says one doctor. "At $100 a sample, once or twice a week over a year or two, that's great mad money."

Babies as Commodities

Payments to donors raise other questions beyond possible physical and psychological risks. Those opposing payment claim that the money makes the eggs and sperm, and the resulting children, commodities. They believe that marketing sperm and eggs is a form of consumer-driven eugenics. Is there a moral difference between designing children for a specific eugenic purpose and designing children according to the whims of the market? Both practices turn children into products of deliberate design.

A survey of younger adults who had been conceived through sperm donation indicated that large minorities were troubled both by "the circumstances of my conception" and the fact that "money was exchanged in order to conceive me." Donor-conceived children are more likely to oppose payments than most Americans.

A large minority said that if a friend were thinking of having a baby by gamete donation, they "would encourage her not to do it."

Many nations have ended the practice of payment for eggs; the United States is the main exception. "We are selling children," says one professor. Critics argue that the traditional idea of "child as gift" is in danger of being replaced with the concept of "child as consumer item," to be purchased in the same way the parents might shop for a computer. An online search for "egg donor" produces countless links. For an example, one advertisement from a clinic reads:

> *We have made a huge effort to provide a large selection of screened donors. They are primarily recruited from colleges and suburban communities, including many young women with Doctoral level educations. Information available to you on all donors includes physical characteristics (height, weight, hair color and type, body build, and blood type), ethnic background, educational record, occupation, special interests, audio interviews, childhood photos and since 2004, adult photos. You can view our donor list online.*

Another problem with the commodification of fertility is that it favors the wealthy. Costs for in vitro fertilization (IVF) and preimplantation genetic diagnosis (PGD) can be high, and insurance coverage may not be available. It is difficult to assure fair and equal access to such expensive technology.

Critics complain that if parents can choose and then pay for their child's traits, perhaps babies who have less than desirable features will not be welcome. Many prospective IVF/PGD users want donors who look and behave like the person they dream of parenting, even though there is no guarantee that the child will be the same way. There may be a tendency among these parents to believe that as consumers, they should—and will—receive the products they ordered and purchased. "The implication is that a child is not worthy of love and acceptance unless he or she fits the image profile," says one analyst. Still, there is no evidence that children born or selected through IVF or PGD are less loved.

Supporters note that while, theoretically, reproduction should not be viewed as part of the marketplace, to assume that it isn't is unrealistic. The baby business is alive and growing. "It's hard to imagine that we could ever put this particular genie back in its bottle," writes one commentator. "Moreover, it's not at all clear that we should. For the baby business produces a good that is inherently good. It produces children, for people who want them."

Struggling with Identity

In many countries in which IVF is part of national health care plans, "identity-release programs" are part of the donation process. This means that offspring can contact the donors upon reaching the age of eighteen. (Egg donors are far less likely to be anonymous than sperm donors.)

In the United States, most sperm donors prefer to remain fully anonymous. For example, out of 136 donors at a New England sperm bank, only 38 chose to have their identities released. One man received $80 a sample but turned down twice as much money if it meant he would become a known donor: "Frankly … I just wasn't comfortable kind of with this idea of having some random kid kind of tracking me down."

Major American sperm banks defend the practice of anonymous donation. They argue that the end of anonymity would lead to a decline in the supplies of donor sperm. This appears to be the case in some European countries that have made anonymous sperm donation illegal (although there is dispute). Anonymous donations are also easier for sperm banks to handle since they do not have to store donor information for years.

However, the practice of anonymous donation is slowly coming under pressure in the United States. The push for openness partially comes from the curiosity some feel about their genetic roots. There is also a medical aspect. If a child falls ill, a family may need more information about his or her paternal genetic heritage than an outdated donor profile could provide.

Many women who are sperm recipients like the idea of donor anonymity because they would prefer to keep the donor completely out of the picture. Yet years later, some recipients regret not having chosen a known donor, especially when the child desperately wants to know more about his or her father.

Some donor-conceived children complain of the lack of information about the biological father. In interviews, they say that it feels as if the anonymity process has deprived them of half their family, half their medical history, and in a sense, half their identity. "I realized I really didn't know half of who I was," said Laura McInnes, who found out she was the daughter of an anonymous sperm donor when she was sixteen years old.

However, with the help of new technologies, including online databases and mail-in DNA tests such as 23andme.com and Ancestry.com, more children have been able to track down these anonymous donors—as well as half-siblings conceived by the same donor. McInnes was able to track down her biological father in this way. "I don't think it is right to keep people away from their biological family, or at least not let them know," McInnes told CBC News in Canada.

Erin Jackson didn't find out she was conceived with donated sperm until she was in her mid-thirties. She called the news "the most significant thing that's happened to me in my entire life." And she agreed with McInnes that more transparency is necessary: "I think anyone that donates sperm should understand that they're making people … and that those people have a right to know where they come from."

With the advent of easier-to-access DNA testing, that kind of transparency may be inevitable. "I think it's folly to be promising anonymity to any kind of donor," Sherry Levitan, a lawyer whose focus is on assisted reproductive technology, told CBC News in 2018.

Donor Records

The parents of adopted children are often anonymous as well. However, in most cases, the machinery of adoption is far more heavily regulated and oriented toward the welfare of the child than is the case with sperm and egg donation.

One of the major differences between adoption and donation is open versus closed record-keeping. Open adoption allows identifying information to be exchanged between adoptive and biological parents, and sometimes between kin and the adopted person. Closed adoption seals all identifying information, barring almost all disclosure. Open adoption is the rule in most countries, and adopted children usually have the right to access their birth records for medical information. Yet in the United States, no laws require the permanent maintenance of official records concerning sperm and egg donor conceptions.

According to one study, donor-conceived Americans are twice as likely as adoptees to report envying peers who know their biological parents. They are also twice as likely to worry that their parents might have lied to them about important matters and three times as likely to feel "confused about who is a member of my family and who is not."

In 2008, Olivia Pratten, the twenty-six-year-old daughter of an anonymous sperm donor, filed a class-action lawsuit against a Canadian clinic for having destroyed records that could have

Olivia Pratten, the daughter of an anonymous sperm donor, filed a lawsuit in Canada insisting that donor records should be kept long-term. She ultimately lost the suit.

identified her biological father. Pratten argued that Canadian law requires the long-term preservation of adoption records but requires records relating to a gamete donor to be preserved for only six years. She claimed this differential treatment discriminated against the children of sperm and egg donors. Pratten noted that once the records are destroyed, a person cannot learn about racial, cultural, and religious history and other important parts of their identity. This irreparable gap causes psychological distress for donor-conceived children. Pratten's attorneys also argued that "if the donor records are lost or destroyed, that information will be lost for all time and Olivia's health and safety could be compromised as a result." Pratten lost the case, and the Canadian Supreme Court refused to hear it.

In the United States, adoption law differs from state to state. Many states do not allow an adult adopted person to receive or even look at a copy of his or her original birth certificate by simply applying to do so. When it comes to donor-conceived children, there has been a move toward more transparency. In 2011, Washington State made "open" sperm donation, in which information about the donor is available to the child, a default. Sperm donors in that state are now required to request anonymity. Washington, however, remains the only US state to have such a law on the books.

Many sperm banks have their own rules about how they keep and share donor information, but in the absence of federal legislation on the matter, many donor-conceived children have supported an official or unofficial donor registry to make it easier for them (as well as donors) to establish contact with genetic kin. In most registry schemes, a donor-conceived person can receive the ID number of the donor from the fertility clinic. If that donor has donated before, then other people with the same donor number are genetic half-siblings. Thus, registry schemes usually make it possible for a person to contact others with whom they share a parent.

The Donor Sibling Registry, a worldwide organization founded in 2000, is probably the largest registry. It has more than sixty thousand members and has connected more than sixteen thousand half-siblings and donors. In recent years, there has been some pressure in the United States to create an official national registry of donor-conceived births, but none has been created to date.

In countries such as the United Kingdom, Germany, and Sweden, donations where the donor's name could never be released have been outlawed. In fact, as of a 2005 law, the Human Fertilisation and Embryology Authority (HFEA) in the UK can give identifying information, including name and address, of a donor to any child when he or she reaches the age of eighteen.

Donation and the Law

In the United States, laws regarding marriage, divorce, child custody, and adoption are usually left to individual states. This

Sperm donor Daryl Hendrix sued Samantha Harrington in Kansas in an attempt to claim parental rights over the twins born to Harrington.

has been the model for rules affecting sperm and egg donation, although the former remains more regulated than the latter. The legal field is trying to keep up with new developments in reproductive technology, and major issues remain unsettled. Rules regarding reproductive technology vary widely from state to state, leaving a confusing patchwork of regulations and laws.

In general, a sperm donor provides the biological material for conception but gives up all legal rights over the children produced from his sperm. At the other extreme, US laws also usually protect sperm donors from responsibilities in connection with children produced from their donations. These laws, which essentially isolate sperm donors from their biological children, are intended to protect the stability of families conceived with donor sperm.

However, some court cases around the globe have been ruling on such protections. On the one hand, some sperm and egg donors have tried to claim parental rights. In 2007, Kansas resident Daryl Hendrix filed a lawsuit against longtime friend

Samantha Harrington, who had given birth to twins conceived by means of his sperm. A divided Kansas Supreme Court ruled 4 to 2 that without a written agreement, sperm donors were not legal parents and did not possess parental rights. "My heart is broken," he said. "Someday these children are going to know I'm their father. We're not finished." Hendrix appealed to the US Supreme Court, which declined to hear the case.

The Supreme Court of Ireland, in the controversial case of *McD v. L* (2009), granted a sperm donor visitation rights to a child born via artificial insemination. The donor had been a friend of the lesbian couple to whom he donated sperm in 2006. However, the trio subsequently argued, and the women attempted to relocate to Australia. The donor obtained an injunction to prevent the women from leaving the country. He then sought legal guardianship of the child. One bioethicist says of the ruling that it "defies both reason and modernity [and] has set family law back a generation."

Distinct from cases dealing with parental rights, on the issue of parental responsibility, some courts have ruled on the financially responsibility of donors. A court in Washington State ruled in 2004 that a donor did not have to pay child support unless he and the mother had a signed contract. However, in 2007, a Pennsylvania court found a sperm donor responsible for supporting his two biological children.

In England, Andy Bathie, a firefighter from North London, provided sperm to Sharon and Terri Arnold after they had assured him that he would have no personal or financial involvement with the children. Two children were born, a boy and a girl. Later, the Arnolds split up, and a British court forced Bathie to pay child support even though he had no legal rights over the boy and girl in question. "I did look into the legal side and understood that, as a couple, they would be the parents, not me. I was never 'daddy,'" Bathie said. According to a representative for the HFEA, men who donated sperm through licensed fertility clinics were not the legal fathers of any children born as a result. However, "men giving out their sperm in any other way, such as internet arrangements, are legally the father of any children born, with all the responsibilities that carries."

While the law is still murky on sperm donation, several general conclusions can be drawn. Sperm donor procedures at licensed fertility clinics include legal contracts intended to prevent subsequent paternity and child support disputes. The courts have upheld these documents. In the absence of a very specifically worded legal contract, though, these protections may not extend to men who donate sperm as part of a personal arrangement.

Legal cases in the United States have helped lead to the continuation of anonymous sperm and egg donation. Men and women hesitate to disclose their contact information when they donate if it might mean even partial financial responsibility for the child later on. One sperm donor explains why he insisted on his anonymity: "The consequences for donors are absolutely catastrophic. If you get found out, you can lose your house, your livelihood. I've never put myself forward as a father—I'm not a dad, I'm just a donor."

Talking with the Child

IVF shares with adoption the question of when to tell the child of a donor parent how he or she was conceived. Most experts agree that delayed disclosure or nondisclosure of donor conception is potentially damaging for children. Yet some recipients do not tell the child that he or she was conceived by means of sperm or egg donation—or they wait until the child is older. With the increasing use of reproductive technology, many children are growing up to discover that one of their parents is not biologically related to them. Psychologists note that this may cause a lasting sense of imbalance and feeling of loss of control.

IVF and Consent

In 2000, Natallie Evans and Howard Johnston became engaged. The next year, Evans found out she had ovarian cancer and undertook IVF before undergoing medical treatment that would make her infertile. Evans's eggs were fertilized with Johnston's sperm, and six of the embryos were frozen and placed in storage. In May 2002, the couple broke up and Johnston requested that the clinic destroy the stored embryos. The law on IVF in Great Britain states that both the man and the woman have to give their consent for IVF to continue. It also

After Natallie Evans (*left*) and Howard Johnston ended their engagement, Evans sued to preserve embryos fertilized with his sperm.

allows either party to withdraw that consent until the time of embryo implantation. Evans refused to consent and began a legal challenge to preserve the embryos.

Attorneys for Evans argued before the British High Court of Justice that once IVF treatment began, the man should not have the right to stop it. Evans's position was that Johnston had already consented to the embryos' creation, storage, and use, and he should not be allowed to change his mind.

Johnston contended that once his relationship with Evans ended, he no longer wanted to start a family with her. Johnston sympathized with Evans's medical problems, but if a child were born, he would be legally, financially, emotionally, and morally responsible for it.

In 2003, the judge ruled against Evans, noting that it was up to Parliament, rather than the High Court, to decide whether the law in this area needed to be changed. Evans then appealed to the European Court of Human Rights (ECHR) in Germany. In 2007, the ECHR ruled 5 to 2 against Evans. The decision stated, "The Court, like the national courts, had great sympathy for the plight of the applicant who, if implantation did not take place, would be deprived of the ability to give birth to her own child." However, the majority found that, even in such exceptional circumstances, the right to a family life could not override Johnston's withdrawal of consent.

In one study of donor conception in single-mother families, about two-thirds of the mothers had not yet disclosed the donor conception to their children. Yet almost all claimed they fully intended to do so at some time in the future. More than three-quarters of the mothers reported being concerned about the psychological and social development of the child, the possibility of genetic disorders, and the lack of access to genetic information when needed. However, the tendency to postpone the discussion reveals the difficulty the mothers faced in finding an appropriate way of sharing the information about the conception with their children.

Research suggests that both adopted and donor-conceived children do best emotionally if told about their genetic origins at an early age. In one study, most people informed in adulthood reported more feelings of confusion and betrayal than were cited by a third of children told at age eleven or younger. Children who find out after a long period of secrecy are most angered by the fact that information has been kept from them. Those told later in life reported more negative feelings regarding their donor conception than those told earlier.

Laboratory Mix-up

IVF raises many complex issues, but in the end, human error may be as intractable a problem as questions of morality. For example, in several cases, doctors have misidentified gametes or transferred the wrong embryos. This has led to legal actions against IVF providers, as well as challenging paternity suits. The true extent of the problem is not clear. For example, one white mother gave birth to African American twins as a result of a laboratory mix-up. She would not have known about the mix-up had it not been for the discrepancy in expected skin color.

In another curious case, the embryo implanted in a forty-eight-year-old woman in California had been mistakenly fertilized

Matthew White (*center*), a child of IVF, used IVF to father his children. White's mother's doctor used his own sperm without permission.

with another woman's husband's sperm. Although the doctor realized his error within minutes of the procedure, he did not inform the newly pregnant woman. An anonymous tip revealed the cover-up after the baby was born. A California court awarded the mother $1 million in damages, but the couple who should have received the embryo sued for custody of the little boy. A family court in California granted the husband twice-weekly access to the child because of the man's status as the biological father. The woman who bore the child, meanwhile, has been granted temporary custody. The case underlines the lack of clear legal or ethical codes to protect IVF clients from such random mishaps.

Because of mistakes like this, many clinics have established procedures to reduce the risk of such mix-ups. Some clinics now require a double witnessing system, where two people check the identity of specimens every time the materials are transferred. However, double witnessing is expensive and time-consuming. Some laboratories have tried technological solutions such as tagging individual specimen containers with uniquely numbered, machine-readable radiofrequency identification (RFID) tags. The lab's computer then tracks specimens throughout the process.

As with all reproductive technologies, new innovations will lead to new ethical quandaries. As personal DNA testing becomes more popular and easy, the landscape of semen and egg donation may change dramatically in the coming years.

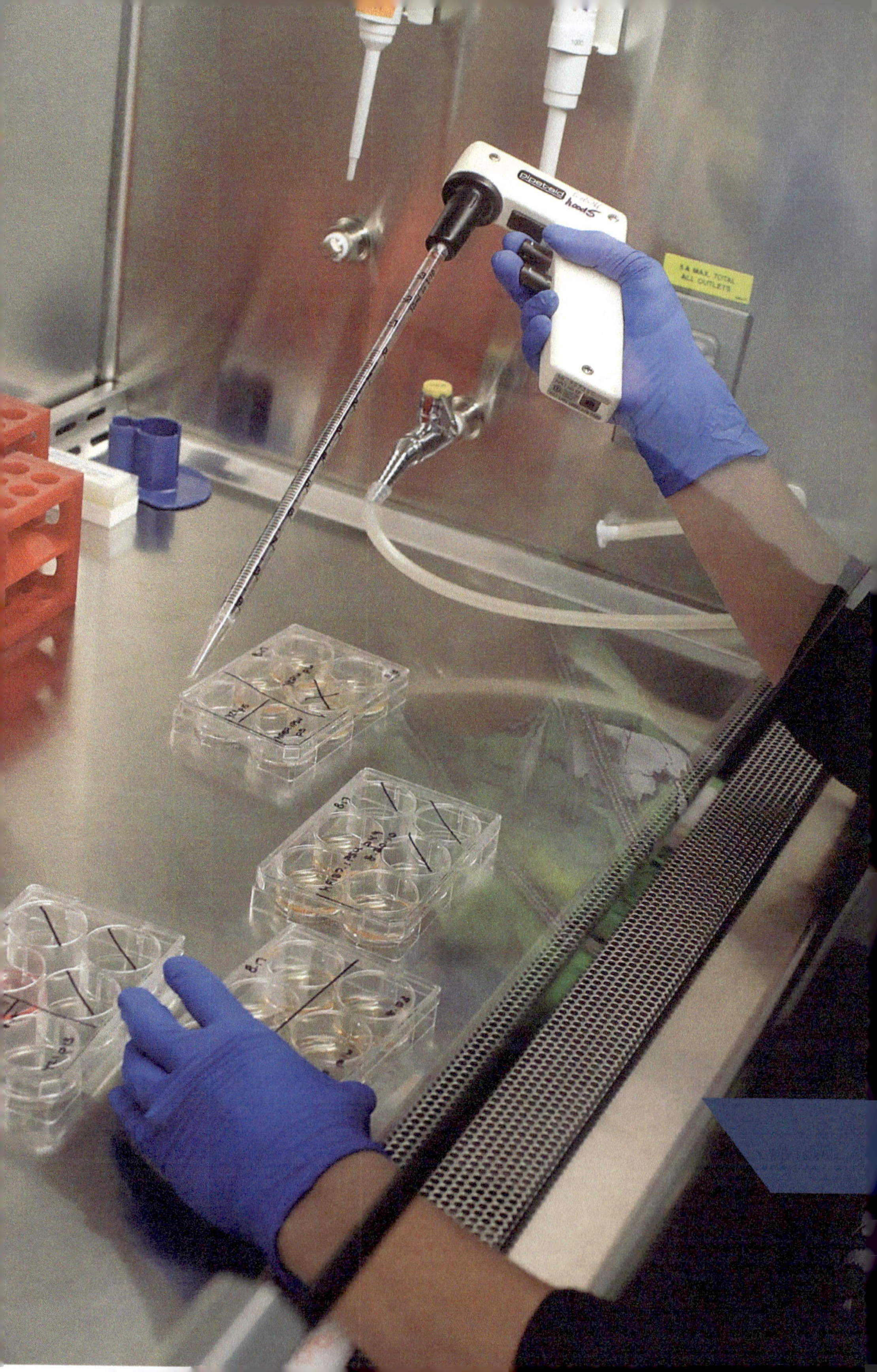
pipetaid
hood5
5 A MAX. TOTAL
ALL OUTLETS

Chapter Six

THE ETHICAL DEBATES CONTINUE

Most new technologies bring with them both the promise of a better future and new challenges to address. Online shopping has made finding what you want more convenient than ever, but it has also eliminated countless retail jobs. Smartphones have made finding information and keeping up with friends easier than ever, but some argue they've hurt our attention spans. The same holds true for reproductive technologies: with each new breakthrough, we can also expect bumps in the road.

Consider, for example, how the mapping of the human genome has changed the landscape of reproduction. About 22,000 human genes control all human hereditary traits. In 1990, the US

Opposite: Stem cells at the University of Connecticut's Stem Cell Institute are fed in 2010.

Department of Energy and the National Institutes of Health began an international effort to identify every one of those genes and determine the sequences of the three billion chemical base pairs that make up human DNA.

In 2006, Human Genome Project researchers announced that they had completed the DNA sequencing of the last of the twenty-four human chromosomes. As a result, the entire collection of DNA sequences appearing in human chromosomes is now stored in databases and accessible to researchers around the world.

The completion of the Human Genome Project has made the genetic basis of some diseases clearer, and progress on genetic manipulation is probably inevitable as well. Genetic advances may make it possible not only to cure diseases but also to enhance muscles, memories, and moods; to choose the sex, height, and other genetic traits of children; and to improve physical and intellectual capacities. The dilemma is that this new knowledge—along with other breakthroughs—may also enable people to manipulate the nature of humanity to an extent now unknown and unforeseeable.

Challenges Ahead

In the short term, complex problems over specific reproductive technology issues continue to arise. For example, US state courts are struggling with legal issues over IVF, such as what should happen to frozen embryos when divorce breaks up couples who had planned to have children together. American involvement in wars in Iraq and Afghanistan has also led to questions over whether children conceived with the frozen sperm of fathers who died before the children were born can share inheritance and life insurance payments with siblings conceived while both parents were alive.

These are difficult questions. In the long term, certain additional issues probably will continue to arise regardless of the technology. For example, who should regulate the use of new reproductive technologies? Some support governmental regulations and restrictions. Others would prefer to have responsibility for making those decisions lie with professional organizations, such as those involved in reproductive medicine. Some argue that neither doctors nor governments should impose their value judgments directly or indirectly on people's behavior in private matters.

A second problem is access to reproductive technology. Fertility is undeniably a business. Clinics earn profits, advertise their expertise, and compete against one another over the quality and success rate of the service they offer—the production of babies. Some people complain that reproductive technology is a waste of expensive and scarce medical resources when it does not address any life-threatening issues. Others fear that babies have been turned into just one more commodity in a consumer-oriented society.

The status of embryos will continue to remain an issue, especially as long as the Roman Catholic Church stands in opposition to in vitro fertilization (IVF) and preimplantation genetic diagnosis (PGD). Even on research using embryos, the church is adamant: "No objective, even though noble in itself, such as a foreseeable advantage to science, to other human beings or to society, can in any way justify experimentation on living human embryos or fetuses, whether viable or not, either inside or outside the mother's womb." Is it ethical to create embryos that will never be developed? What should be done with frozen embryos as they lose their viability?

A few studies have shown that IVF babies have an increased risk of health complications, birth defects, and developmental disorders over children conceived in the traditional way. Other studies seem to contradict these findings. Since the IVF procedure is only forty years old, it may be another few decades before data about children who have been brought into the world by technology can be properly interpreted.

A final concern involves the hubris at the core of all reproductive technology. Many people believe that any change from natural procreation to reproductive technology is harmful to individuals and, if it were to become widespread, would also harm society.

Stem Cell Research Debate

In the United States, the strength of the antiabortion movement will continue to have a major effect on certain aspects of reproductive technology. For example, arguments over the status of the human embryo have made human embryonic stem cell research an extremely controversial issue. The creation of a human embryonic stem cell line often requires the destruction of a human embryo—though in 2006, scientists figured out how to stimulate a patient's own cells to act in the same way. However, some human embryos are still needed for research, and this has opponents up in arms.

Antiabortion activists believe that this type of embryonic stem cell research violates the sanctity of human life. They argue that life begins when a sperm cell fertilizes an egg. Thus a blastocyst—a clump of approximately 150 embryonic cells in the laboratory—is the equivalent of a person.

Opponents of stem cell research claim that research involving embryos is the first step down a slippery slope to embryo farms, cloned babies, the use of fetuses for spare parts, and the commodification of human life. The official position of the Catholic Church is that "human embryos obtained 'in vitro' are human beings and subjects with rights: their dignity and right to

On March 9, 2009, President Barack Obama (*center*) signs an executive order to remove federal funding restrictions on newer stem cell lines.

life must be respected from the first moment of their existence. It is immoral to produce human embryos destined to be exploited as disposable 'biological material.'"

In 2001, President George W. Bush declared that federal funds could be used for embryonic stem cell research on existing stem cell lines only—essentially only the twenty-one stem cell lines created before August 2001. The president stated that taxpayer money would not be allowed to fund the creation of new lines of stem cells.

This limitation on the supply of research materials made it difficult to investigate the properties of stem cells. In 2006 and 2007, Congress passed laws that would have opened up stem cell lines for federally funded research as long as the embryos were left over from IVF fertility treatments. In both cases, President Bush vetoed the bills, saying that he did not want to support "the taking of innocent human life." Nevertheless, he did not seek to ban stem cell research in the private sector.

When Barack Obama became president in 2009, one of his first acts removed the restriction on federal funding for newer stem cell lines. Obama's reversal allowed researchers to use hundreds of stem cell lines already in existence as well as any further lines created by using private funds or state-level funding. However, as of 2018, US law still banned federally funded "research in which a human embryo or embryos are destroyed, discarded, or knowingly subjected to risk of injury or death." This ban, called the Dickey-Wicker Amendment, nonetheless lived in something of a legal gray area, with some types of research involving embryos having been ruled permissible.

It is possible that this particular issue will fade out altogether. Scientists have tried to reprogram mature cells to make them just as potent as stem cells. These are known as induced pluripotent stem cells, abbreviated as iPS cells. Researchers first produced iPS cells from mice in 2006 and from humans in 2007. The induced cells are similar to natural embryonic stem cells in many respects but they are not identical, and the differences are still not clear. The use of iPS cells may yet allow researchers to obtain a useful variety of stem cells without the controversial use of embryos. However, as of 2018, biologist Shinya Yamanaka told the journal *Nature* that "[t]he importance of human ES [embryonic stem] cells is no less now than 20 years ago, and I do not imagine it will be any lower in the future."

Stem cells can also be obtained by using somatic cell nuclear transfer (SCNT) technology. This technique, commonly referred to as therapeutic cloning, involves removing the DNA from an egg and replacing it with the DNA from another cell that has been removed from an individual of the same species. The resulting embryo is allowed to grow for about fourteen days, then its stem cells are extracted and grown to produce a piece of tissue or a complete organ for transplant. The resulting entity would be a perfect genetic match and would not trigger a reaction from the host immune system. However, even this limited form of cloning would face strong opposition if applied to clone complete human beings.

Cloning Humans

Some of the reproductive technology in use today could eventually enable human cloning. People are fascinated by the idea that a person might someday be able to generate a near-genetic replica of himself or herself. The process, known as reproductive cloning, has become a staple of science fiction and a much-debated topic in philosophical circles.

Reproductive cloning attempts to use SCNT technology to produce a living genetic duplicate of the original organism. The issue burst into the world's consciousness as a real possibility in 1996 with the creation of Dolly, a cloned sheep. Dolly was the first mammal cloned by means of SCNT from an adult somatic cell. Since Dolly, researchers have cloned other large mammals, including horses, bulls, and a dog. The "production" of Dolly proved that genes in a mature, differentiated somatic cell can still revert to an embryonic state, causing behavior like that of an undifferentiated cell. Scientists could then induce the cell to develop into any part of an animal or even re-create a whole individual.

Most of the commentary in the mid-1990s was concerned not with Dolly herself but rather with the possibility of human cloning and its implications for human welfare. In the view of a bioethicist who testified to Congress, "Human cloning is immoral ... Human cloning constitutes unethical experimentation on the cloned-child-to-be. It confounds his genetic and social identity; it would threaten his sense of individuality. It represents a giant step toward turning procreation into manufacture. And it is a despotic attempt by parents to select and control the genetic make-up of their children."

On the other hand, Ian Wilmut, the English embryologist who helped produce Dolly the sheep, argued that it would be ethical to extend cloning technology to human embryos. The technology could help derive treatments to repair a person's own

Dolly: The Cloning of a Sheep, 1996

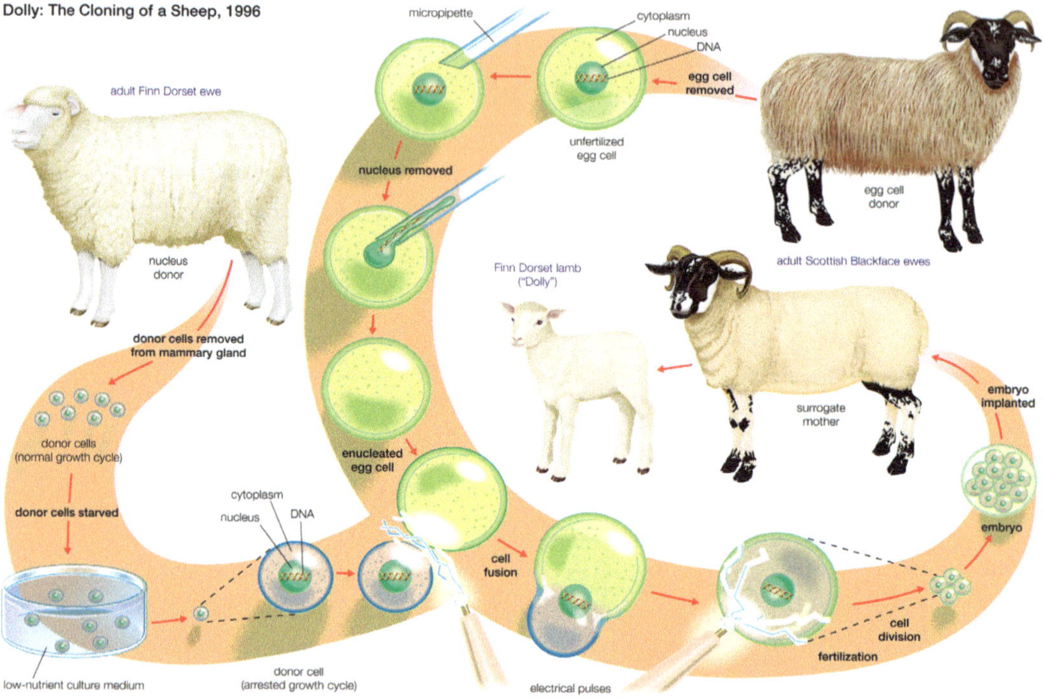

This chart shows the complicated process by which a sheep named Dolly was successfully cloned in the 1990s.

body and might someday be used to correct hereditary defects at the embryo stage, which would allow healthy development. "One day doctors will be able to use cloning to grow a patient's own cells and tissues to carry out repairs … The potential of cloning to alleviate human suffering—even end it for some diseases—is so great in the medium term that I believe it would be immoral not to clone human embryos for treatments."

Human reproductive cloning remains an unproven and uncertain technology. Animal experiments with cloning have had uneven results. Many miscarriages have occurred, and live offspring have frequently shown signs of premature aging and genetic disorders. In fact, Dolly, the only lamb that survived to adulthood from 277 cloning attempts, was only six years old when she died. Sheep usually live to be eleven or twelve.

Polls show strong opposition to cloning. In 2018, 40 percent of Americans thought that cloning animals was morally acceptable, and only 16 percent thought cloning humans was acceptable, according to Gallup. Still, both numbers were higher than they had ever been since 2001, when the Gallup poll began. President Barack Obama said in 2009 that he had designed his stem cell policy so that it "never opens the door to the use of cloning for human reproduction. Such cloning is dangerous, profoundly wrong, and has no place in our society or any society."

Yet, what exactly is wrong with creating a child who is a genetic twin of his or her parent, or of an older sibling who has tragically died, or of an admired scientist, sports star, or celebrity? Many bioethicists believe it is only a matter of time before someone successfully clones a human being. Whether public opinion will change at that point is an open question.

The Surrogacy Debate

More people are going outside of their own countries to look for lower-cost surrogacy options. While a typical surrogacy for American clients can cost more than $100,000, the cost can be cut by two-thirds by going to Ukraine or Laos to find a surrogate.

As this practice has become more common, the debate around ethical practices in surrogacy has amplified. Surrogacy is illegal in many European countries, so many have sought surrogates in Asia. Now, those countries are restricting the practice, too. Paying a surrogate became illegal in Thailand in 2015, and it was banned outright in Nepal. India, where a growing industry had been built around surrogacy for foreigners, made such surrogacy illegal.

The argument for making this practice illegal is that many women who are poor, illiterate, and unable to find other work

Fatherless Birth

In an ironic twist, new developments in reproductive technology may make the male and his sperm superfluous in reproduction. For example, scientists are approaching the point of being able to achieve parthenogenesis (from the Greek, indicating "virgin birth"). In biology, parthenogenesis is a form of reproduction in which an egg develops into a new individual without any fertilization at all. Since there is no involvement of a male gamete, parthenogenesis often leads to the production of offspring that are genetically identical to the mother.

Natural parthenogenesis exists in many animals, such as rotifers and aphids. In some social insects, such as the honeybee and the ant, unfertilized eggs give rise to male drones and fertilized eggs to female workers and queens. Parthenogenesis has also been observed in some snakes, fish, and monitor lizards. The phenomenon is rarer among plants (where it is called parthenocarpy), but it can be found in species of roses and orange trees.

In 1900, Jacques Loeb accomplished the first clear case of artificial parthenogenesis when he demonstrated that unfertilized frog eggs, upon being pricked with a needle, sometimes went on to exhibit normal embryonic development. Researchers have since induced parthenogenesis in almost all major groups of animals. In 1936, Gregory Pincus, later one of the developers of the birth control pill, claimed to have induced parthenogenesis in rabbit eggs. In 2004, scientists in Tokyo used parthenogenesis to create a fatherless mouse.

People have always believed that human births from parthenogenesis were unlikely. Induced parthenogenesis in mice and monkeys often results in abnormal development; it has seemed doubtful that anyone would take a chance on producing humans in this way.

However, the process can create human embryos for experimentation. The discredited South Korean scientist Hwang Woo-Suk accidentally achieved this result in 2007. Although Hwang deceived the world by asserting that he had performed the first human cloning, his group was the first to succeed in performing human parthenogenesis to create viable embryos. If this procedure could be performed cheaply and effectively, the ability to extract embryonic stem cells produced by parthenogenesis would mean that extracted cells could be created that were genetically identical to the egg donor. The process may offer a way of creating stem cells (without cloning) that could be used in the treatment of degenerative diseases in women.

are being exploited by questionable business practices and low wages within these industries. For instance, some had multiple embryos implanted with the goal of making pregnancy more likely but without being told the risks associated with a multiple pregnancy (a pregnancy involving more than one baby). Proper care after birth wasn't always available, and the Caesarean section procedure during the birthing process was often used too much, an article in the *Economist* reported.

These bans haven't stopped the surrogacy business from thriving. As the *Economist* confirmed in 2017:

> *[T]he business is shifting to Greece, Laos and Ukraine, says Sam Everingham of Families Through Surrogacy, an Australian charity. Several African countries are becoming more popular; Indian women seeking to be surrogates are going to Kenya. Far from their families and friends, and unable to speak the local language, they are more vulnerable to exploitation and abuse.*

Legislation around surrogacy, meanwhile, remains hard to navigate in some countries. In the United Kingdom, for example, it was—until 2017—illegal for single people to contract with surrogates, so many would go abroad to find surrogates. However, when they returned to the UK with their babies, they often encountered difficulties being recognized as the legal parents of the children or getting the children citizenship. This remains a problem for most Britons who go abroad seeking surrogates.

Looking Ahead

How far are we from Aldous Huxley's fertilizing and decanting rooms in the Central London Hatchery in *Brave New World*? Huxley himself wrote a nonfiction sequel, *Brave New World*

Revisited, in 1958. In this small collection of essays, he concluded that in the twenty-six years since he wrote the original book, the real world was becoming more like his bestseller at a much faster rate than he had imagined in the 1930s. Yet in *Brave New World Revisited*, Huxley had almost nothing to say about reproductive technology except for expressing vague fears about the "progressive contamination of the genetic pool," a sentiment of the eugenics movement. Huxley died in 1963; had he lived until 1978, when the first IVF baby was created, he almost certainly would have had more to say about the new ways for humans to reproduce.

It is likely that only an international ban, an extremely unlikely outcome, could ever stop reproductive technology from spreading. Without an international ban, some assert, one country will use the latest advances in reproductive technology and all other nations will follow suit. The same line of reasoning can be applied on a personal level. Nobel Prize winner James Watson notes, "Once you have a way in which you can improve our children, no one can stop it. It would be stupid not to use it because someone else will. Those parents who enhance their children, then their children are going to be the ones who dominate the world."

The "no one can stop it" argument is impossible to disprove, in the same way that a "slippery slope" argument is. Perhaps because they cannot be falsified, these argument have become a default position for many advocates of and opponents to the use of reproductive technology.

It is worthwhile to try to predict the future, as Huxley did, since it can help to prevent us from making grave mistakes. At the same time, with reproductive technologies advancing so quickly, it is impossible to predict all the implications and ramifications of their use. So the ethical debate continues in lockstep with scientific developments. This, perhaps, is the only way to discover an ethically sound way forward.

Glossary

abstinence The practice of restraining oneself from sexual intercourse.

adultery Sexual intercourse between a person who is married and someone who is not his or her spouse.

amniocentesis The insertion of a needle into the uterus to withdraw amniotic fluid.

amniotic fluid The liquid substance that surrounds an embryo or fetus in the uterus.

blastocyst A spherical mass of about 150 cells.

Caesarean section A surgical procedure during birth in which the baby is extracted via an incision in the uterus rather than through the vaginal canal.

commodity An economic good; something that can usually be bought or sold.

conception The process of becoming pregnant.

contraception Intentional prevention of conception by means of medicine or other methods.

engender To cause to exist; to conceive a child.

eugenics The practice of selective breeding among humans in order to "improve" their genetic makeup.

fallopian tubes The pair of tubes through which eggs travel from the ovary to the uterus.

fecundity Fertility; fruitfulness in offspring.

feticide The act of killing a fetus.

fetus An unborn and developing human still in a mother's womb.

infanticide The act of killing a baby.

menopause A biological process in which women lose the ability to have a child in their forties or fifties.

ovulation The expulsion of an egg from the ovary.

prenatal Before the birth of a baby; during pregnancy.

procreation The act of reproduction, or producing offspring.

semen A fluid in the male reproductive tract that contains sperm.

sperm The male reproductive cell.

sterilization The act of depriving someone of the ability to reproduce.

ultrasound A diagnostic examination used to produce images of the inside of the body, often used to retrieve images of a fetus.

uterus An organ inside animals of the female sex in which a fetus grows and develops before birth.

vulcanization The process of treating rubber or some plastics chemically for the purpose of making them useful.

Further Information

Books

Ballard, Carol. *Understanding Reproduction* (Understanding the Human Body). New York: Rosen Central, 2010.

Lew, Kristi. *Human Cloning* (Sci-Fi or STEM?). New York: Rosen Young Adult, 2018.

Oransky Wittenstein, Vicki. *Reproductive Rights: Who Decides?* Minneapolis, MN: Twenty-First Century Books, 2016.

Ross, Loretta. *Reproductive Justice: An Introduction* (Reproductive Justice: A New Vision for the 21st Century). Oakland, CA: University of California Press, 2017.

Websites

Donor Sibling Registry

https://www.donorsiblingregistry.com

This organization, founded in 2000, has more than 61,000 members and has connected upwards of 16,354 half-siblings and donors to date.

National Institutes of Health: Stem Cell Information

http://stemcells.nih.gov

This website offers a wealth of information on stem cell research, how it is funded, and the latest scientific findings. It also includes the NIH Human Embryonic Stem Cell Registry, which logs which stem cell lines are permissible for utilization in NIH-funded research.

WebMD Infertility & Reproduction Health Center

https://www.webmd.com/infertility-and-reproduction/default.htm

From causes and symptoms to treatment and solutions, this website offers a comprehensive overview of what infertility is and how it's being addressed.

Videos

Introduction to Genetic Engineering

https://www.khanacademy.org/science/high-school-biology/hs-molecular-genetics/hs-biotechnology/v/introduction-to-genetic-engineering

This Khan Academy video explains the history of genetic engineering and how it works.

Reproductive Technologies: Definition, Examples & Risks

https://study.com/academy/lesson/reproductive-technologies-definition-examples-risks.html

This animated video is an introduction to assisted reproductive technology, explaining three different methods.

3D Animation of How IVF Works

https://www.youtube.com/watch?v=GeigYib39Rs

This video shows a fascinating three-dimensional animation of ovulation, egg fertilization, and the in vitro fertilization process.

Organizations

American Pregnancy Association

3007 Skyway Circle N., Suite 800

Irving, TX 75038

(800) 672-2296

http://americanpregnancy.org/infertility

The fertility page of the American Pregnancy Association's website offers information on sperm banks and collecting sperm, in vitro fertilization, fertility testing, and more.

American Society for Reproductive Medicine

1209 Montgomery Highway

Birmingham, AL 35216-2809

(205) 978-5000

https://www.asrm.org

The ASRM is an organization that provides and collects a variety of education and research materials on reproductive medicine.

Centers for Disease Control and Prevention

1600 Clifton Road

Atlanta, GA 30329-4027

(800) 232-4636

https://www.cdc.gov/art/index.html

The CDC's web page on assisted reproductive technology offers statistical information and data on success rates of different reproductive technologies and on infertility in the United States.

Fertility Matters Canada

PO Box 30013

Moncton, NB E1C 0N2

Canada

(800) 263-2929

http://fertilitymatters.ca

This national charitable organization in Canada is dedicated to helping people achieve reproductive health.

Human Fertilisation and Embryology Authority

10 Spring Gardens

SW1A 2BU London

United Kingdom

+44 020 7291 8200

https://www.hfea.gov.uk

This British governmental department offers a guide for all types of families and all types of people looking to learn more about fertility.

Public Health Agency of Canada

130 Colonnade Road

A.L. 6501H

Ottawa, ON K1A 0K9

Canada

(844) 280-5020

https://www.canada.ca/en/public-health/services/fertility/fertility.html

The Public Health Agency of Canada's fertility page offers insights on infertility treatment options, how to cope with stress and potential health risks during treatment, and genetic testing.

Bibliography

"Act for Protection of Embryos [Germany]." *Federal Law Gazette* 69 (December 19, 1990): 2746. http://www.bmj.bund.de/files/-/1147/ESchG%20englisch.pdf.

Adams, Mark, ed. *The Wellborn Science: Eugenics in Germany, France, Brazil, and Russia*. New York: Oxford University Press, 1990.

Ajmani, Sumeet. "North Coast Women's Care: California's Still-Undefined Standard for Protecting Religious Freedom." *California Law Review* 97 (December 2009): 1867–1876. http://www.californialawreview.org/articles/north-coast-women-s-care-california-s-still-undefined-standard-for-protecting-religious-freedom.

Alfonsi, Sharyn. "Inside Egg Donation: More Money for Blondes?" ABC News, May 11, 2010. http://abcnews.go.com/WN/egg-donation-agencies-paid-money-favored-attributes/story?id=10614326.

Ali, Lorraine. "The Curious Lives of Surrogates." *Newsweek*, March 29, 2008. http://www.*newsweek*.com/2008/03/29/the-curious-lives-of-surrogates.html.

American Society for Reproductive Medicine Ethics Committee. "Access to Fertility Treatment by Gays, Lesbians, and Unmarried Persons." *Fertility and Sterility* 92 (October 2009): 1190–1193.

———. "Financial Compensation for Oocyte Donors." *Fertility and Sterility*: 305–309. http://www.asrm.org/uploadedFiles/ASRM_Content/News_and_Publications/Ethics_Committee_Reports_and_Statements/financial_incentives.pdf.

Andrews, Lori. *The Clone Age: Adventures in the New World of Reproductive Technology*. New York: Henry Holt, 2000.

Appel, Jacob. "May Doctors Refuse Infertility Treatments to Gay Patients?" *Hastings Center Report* 36 (July 2006): 20–21. http://www.thehastingscenter.org/Publications/HCR/Detail.aspx?id=1464.

———. "Revenge of the Sperm Donors." *Huffington Post*, December 27, 2009. http://www.huffingtonpost.com/jacob-m-appel/revenge-of-the-sperm-dono_b_404479.html.

———. "Want a Daughter? Try Paying for Her." *Opposing Views*, August 26, 2009. http://www.opposingviews.com/p/want-a-daughter-try-paying-for-her.

"ART and Gestational Carriers: Key Findings—Use of Gestational Carriers in the United States." Centers for Disease Control and Prevention, August 5, 2016. https://www.cdc.gov/art/key-findings/gestational-carriers.html.

"As Demand for Surrogacy Soars, More Countries Are Trying to Ban It." *Economist*, May 13, 2017. https://www.econmist.com/international/2017/05/13/as-demand-for-surrogacy-soars-more-countries-are-trying-to-ban-it.

Ashcroft, Richard. *Principles of Health Care Ethics*. Hoboken, NJ: John Wiley, 2007.

Ayres, Chris. "Mother Wins $1M for IVF Mix-Up but May Lose Son." *London Times*, August 5, 2004. http://www.timesonline.co.uk/tol/news/world/article465773.ece.

Barnhart, Michael. "Nature, Nurture, and No-Self: Bioengineering and Buddhist Values." *Journal of Buddhist Ethics* 7 (2000). http://www.buddhistethics.org/7/barnhart001.html.

Black, Edwin. *War Against the Weak: Eugenics and America's Campaign to Create a Master Race*. New York: Four Walls Eight Windows, 2003.

Brock, D. W. "The Non-identity Problem and Genetic Harms—The Case of Wrongful Handicaps." *Bioethics* 9 (July 1995): 269–275. http://www.ncbi.nlm.nih.gov/pubmed/11653042.

Bruinius, Harry. *Better for All the World: The Secret History of Forced Sterilization and America's Quest for Racial Purity*. New York: Alfred Knopf, 2006.

Buchanan, Allen, et al. *From Chance to Choice: Genetics and Justice*. Cambridge, UK: Cambridge University Press, 2000.

Canada Department of Justice. "Assisted Human Reproduction Act (2004)." http://laws.justice.gc.ca/en/showdoc/cs/A-13.4/bo-ga:s_5/20090616/en#anchorbo-ga:s_5.

Carne, Lucy. "$perm Wail by Donor: Must Pay Support 18 Yrs. Later." *New York Post*, December 2, 2007. http://www.nypost.com/p/news/regional/item_G12JUtb7B01PPOSLtDp5JK;jsessionid=09A7443DD940C34851F96B5A13595515.

"Case of Evans v. the United Kingdom—Judgment." European Court of Human Rights, April 10, 2007. http://cmiskp.echr.coe.int/tkp197/view asp?action=html&documentId=815166&portal=hbkm&source=externalbydocnumber&table=F69A27FD8FB86142BF01C1166DEA398649.

"Catechism of the Catholic Church: Part 3—Life in Christ." Vatican, 1993. http://www.vatican.va/archive/catechism/p3s2c2a6.htm#III.

"CDCs Abortion Surveillance System FAQs." Centers for Disease Control and Prevention, November 19, 2018. https://www.cdc.gov/reproductivehealth/data_stats/abortion.htm.

Center for Genetics and Society. "James Watson's Legacy." *Biopolitical Times*, October 22, 2007. http://www.biopoliticaltimes.org/article.php?id=3723.

"China's One Child Policy." Marketplace, 2010. http://market place.publicradio.org/projects/project_display.php?proj_identifier=2010/06/21/china-one-child-policy.

Choi, Charles. "Cell-Off: Induced Pluripotent Stem Cells Fall Short of Potential Found in Embryonic Version." *Scientific American*, February 11, 2010. http://www.scientificamerican.com/article.cfm?id=cell-induced-pluripotent.

Chung, Emily, Melanie Glanz, and Vik Adhopia. "Donor-Conceived People Are Tracking Down Their Biological Fathers, even if They Want to Hide." CBC News, January 15, 2018. https://www.cbc.ca/news/technology/sperm-donor-dna-testing-1.4500517.

"Cloning." Gallup, May 2018. https://news.gallup.com/poll/6028/cloning.aspx.

"Code of Practice: Embryo Testing and Sex Selection." Human Fertilisation and Embryology Authority, October 2018. https://www.hfea.gov.uk/media/2565/hfea-draft-code-of-practice-9th-edition-consultation-version.pdf.

Cogdell, Christina. *Eugenic Design: Streamlining America in the 1930s.* Philadelphia: University of Pennsylvania Press, 2004.

Cooperman, Alan. "Catholics Split on Embryo Issue: 'Adoption' Embraced by Evangelicals in Stem Cell Debate." *Washington Post*, May 31, 2005. http://www.washingtonpost.com/wp-dyn/content/article/2005/05/30/AR2005053000872.html

"Couple 'Choose' to Have Deaf Baby." BBC, April 8, 2002. http://news.bbc.co.uk/2/hi/health/1916462.stm.

Coward, Harold. "Hinduism, Contemporary Issues in Science and Religion." *Encyclopedia of Science and Religion*, Encyclopedia.com, 2003. https://www.encyclopedia.com/education/encyclopedias-almanacs-transcripts-and-maps/hinduism-contemporary-issues-science-and-religion.

Cyranoski, David. "How Human Embryonic Stem Cells Sparked a Revolution." *Nature*, March 20, 2018. https://www.nature.com/articles/d41586-018-03268-4.

Daniels, Kimberly, Jill Daugherty, and Jo Jones. "Current Contraceptive Status Among Women Aged 15–44: United States, 2011–2013." Centers for Disease Control and Prevention, December 2014. https://www.cdc.gov/nchs/data/databriefs/db173.htm.

"Daughter of Sperm Donor Seeks to Know Identity of Biological Father." *Vancouver Sun*, October 27, 2008. http://www.canada.com/vancouversun/news/story.html?id=3146c8d6-d2a6-4d3b-a911-6eaaa3732558.

Dickens, B. "Can Sex Selection Be Ethically Tolerated?" *Journal of Medical Ethics* 28 (2002): 335–336.

"The Difference Between IUI and IVF." Society for Assisted Reproductive Technology. Accessed November 29, 2018. https://www.sart.org/patients/fyi-videos/the-difference-between-iui-and-ivf.

Dolan, Maura. "Doctors' Faith Must Yield to Gays' Rights, Court Says." *Los Angeles Times*, August 19, 2008. http://articles.latimes.com/2008/aug/19/local/me-supreme19.

Douthat, Ross. "The Birds and the Bees (via the Fertility Clinic)." *New York Times*, May 31, 2010.

Dunlap, David. "Sperm Donor Is Awarded Standing as Girl's Father." *New York Times*, November 19, 1994. http://www.nytimes.com/1994/11/19/nyregion/sperm-donor-is-awarded-standing-as-girl-s-father.html.

Dunn, Leslie, and T. Dobzhansky. *Heredity, Race, and Society*. New York: New American Library, 1952.

Egendorf, Laura. *Should Parents Be Allowed to Choose the Gender of Their Children?* Detroit: Greenhaven Press, 2008.

Ekerhovd E., A. Faurskov, and C. Werner. "Swedish Sperm Donors Are Driven by Altruism, but Shortage of Sperm Donors Leads to Reproductive Traveling." *Upsala Journal of Medical Sciences* 113 (2008): 305–313. http://www.ncbi.nlm.nih.gov/pubmed/18991243.

"Embryo Case: Reaction." BBC News, April 10, 2007. http://news.bbc.co.uk/2/hi/health/6541737.stm#steel.

Eunjung Cha, Ariana. "Discounts, Guarantees and the Search for 'Good' Genes: The Booming Fertility Business." *Washington Post*, October 21, 2017. https://www.washingtonpost.com/national/

health-science/donor-eggs-sperm-banks-and-the-quest-for-good-genes/2017/10/21/64b9bdd0-aaa6-11e7-b3aa-c0e2e1d41e38_story.html?utm_term=.dd4a062cc3fc.

"Facts and Figures." Alzheimer's Association. Accessed November 30, 2018. https://www.alz.org/alzheimers-dementia/facts-figures.

"Female Infertility." US Department of Health and Human Services. Accessed November 29, 2018. https://www.hhs.gov/opa/reproductive-health/fact-sheets/female-infertility/index.html.

Fetters, Ashley. "Finding the Lost Generation of Sperm Donors." *Atlantic*, May 18, 2018. https://www.theatlantic.com/family/archive/2018/05/sperm-donation-anonymous/560588.

Franklin, Robert. "Irish Supreme Court: Child Has Right to Knowledge of and Contact with Both Biological Parents." *Men's News Daily*, December 19, 2009. http://mensnewsdaily.com/glennsacks/2009/12/19/irish-supreme-court-child-has-right-to-knowledge-of-and-contact-with-both-biological-parents.

Freeman, T., et al. "Gamete Donation: Parents' Experiences of Searching for Their Child's Donor Siblings and Donor." *Human Reproduction* 24 (2009): 505–516. http://humrep.oxfordjournals.org/cgi/content/abstract/24/3/505.

Gallagher, Nancy. *Breeding Better Vermonters: The Eugenics Project in the Green Mountain State*. Hanover, NH: University Press of New England, 1999.

Gardner, William. "Can Human Genetic Enhancement be Prohibited?" *Journal of Medicine and* Philosophy 20 (1995): 65–84.

Gaskell, Stephanie. "Better Than Sex? In-Vitro Fertilization Could Be New Favorite Method for Baby Making, Scientists Say." *New York Daily News*, May 17, 2010.

Gavaghan, Colin. *Defending the Genetic Supermarket: Law and Ethics of Selecting the Next Generation.* New York: Routledge, 2008.

Genetics and IVF Institute. https://www.givf.com/index.shtml.

Genetic Science Learning Center. "The Stem Cell Debate: Is It Over?" Learn.Genetics, University of Utah, July 10, 2014. https://learn.genetics.utah.edu/content/stemcells/scissues.

Glass, James. *"Life Unworthy of Life": Racial Phobia and Mass Murder in Hitler's Germany.* New York: Basic Books, 1997.

Glazer, Ellen, and Evelina Sterling. *Having Your Baby Through Egg Donation.* Indianapolis: Perspectives Press, 2005.

Goldberg, Carey. "The Search for DGM 2598." *Boston Globe*, November 23, 2008. http://www.boston.com/news/local/massachusetts/articles/2008/11/23/the_search_for_dgm_2598/?page=1.

Goodkind, Daniel. "Should Prenatal Sex Selection Be Restricted? Ethical Questions and Their Implications for Research and Policy." *Population Studies* 53 (1999): 49–61. http://www.jstor.org/pss/2584811.

Gould, Stephen Jay. "Carrie Buck's Daughter." *Natural History* 93 (July 1984): 14–18. http://findarticles.com/p/articles/mi_m1134/is_6_111/ai_87854861/?tag=content;col1.

———. *The Mismeasure of Man.* New York: W. W. Norton, 1981.

Graham, Jack. "Indian Police Raid Illegal Ultrasound Centres to Save Unborn Girls." *Apolitical*, January 24, 2018. https://apolitical.co/solution_article/indian-police-raid-illegal-ultrasound-centres-save-unborn-girls.

"Guttmacher Statistic on Catholic Women's Contraceptive Use." Guttmacher Institute, February 15, 2012. https://www.guttmacher.org/article/2012/02/guttmacher-statistic-catholic-womens-contraceptive-use.

Haas, John. "Begotten Not Made: A Catholic View of Reproductive Technology." US Conference of Catholic Bishops, 1998. http://www.usccb.org/issues-and-action/human-life-and-dignity/reproductive-technology/begotten-not-made-a-catholic-view-of-reproductive-technology.cfm.

Hackett, Conrad, and David McClendon. "Christians Remain World's Largest Religious Group, but They Are Declining in Europe." Pew Research Center, April 5, 2017. http://www.pewresearch.org/fact-tank/2017/04/05/christians-remain-worlds-largest-religious-group-but-they-are-declining-in-europe.

Haller, Mark. *Eugenics: Hereditarian Attitudes in American Thought*. New Brunswick, NJ: Rutgers University Press, 1963.

Harkness, Kelsey. "Sex Selection Abortions Are Rife in the U.S." *Newsweek*, April 14, 2016. https://www.newsweek.com/sex-selection-abortion-rife-us-447403.

Harmon, Amy. "Burden of Knowledge: Tracking Prenatal Health: In New Tests for Fetal Defects, Agonizing Choices for Parents." *New York Times*, June 20, 2004. http://www.nytimes.com/2004/06/20/us/burden-knowledge-tracking-prenatal-health-new-tests-for-fetal-defects-agonizing.html?pagewanted=1.

———. "The Problem with an Almost-Perfect Genetic World." *New York Times*, November 20, 2005. http://www.nytimes.com/2005/11/20/weekinreview/20harmon.html.

"HFEA to Help Donor-Conceived Siblings Contact Each Other." Human Fertilisation and Embryology Authority, April 6 , 2010. http://www.hfea.gov.uk/5838.html.

"HFEA Horizon Scanning: What's Next for Fertility Treatment and Embryo Research?" Human Fertilisation and Embryology Authority, September 16, 2009. http://www.hfea.gov.uk/5397.html.

Hodin, Sarah. "The Burden of Infertility: Global Prevalence and Women's Voices from Around the World." Maternal Health Task Force, January 18, 2017. https://www.mhtf.org/2017/01/18/the-burden-of-infertility-global-prevalence-and-womens-voices-from-around-the-world.

Hollingsworth, Leslie. "Ethical Considerations in Prenatal Sex Selection." *Health and Social Work* 30 (May 2005): 126–134.

Hooper, Michael. "Sperm Donor Needed Pact, High Court Rules." *Topeka Capital-Journal*, October 27, 2007. http://cjonline.com/stories/102707/sta_212538275.shtml.

Hopkins, Jim. "Egg-Donor Business Booms on Campuses." *USA TODAY*, March 15, 2006. http://www.usatoday.com/money/industries/health/2006-03-15-egg-donors-usat_x.htm.

Hudson, Valerie, and Andrea den Boer. *Bare Branches: The Security Implications of Asia's Surplus Male Population*. Cambridge, MA: M.I.T. Press, 2004.

"Hull Becomes the Latest Clinic to Guard Against IVF Mix Ups." Private Healthcare UK, January 2008. http://www.privatehealth.co.uk/news/january-2008/hull-guards-against-ivf-mix-ups563.

Hurlbut, J. Benjamin, Sheila Jasanoff, and Krishanu Sana. "The Chinese Gene-Editing Experiment Was an Outrage. The Scientific Community Shares Blame." *Washington Post*, November 29, 2018. https://www.washingtonpost.com/outlook/2018/11/29/chinese-gene-editing-experiment-was-an-outrage-broader-scientific-community-shares-some-blame/?utm_term=.d9fcccac2fd3.

Huxley, Aldous. *Brave New World* and *Brave New World Revisited*. New York: Harper Perennial Modern Classics, 2005 [1932, 1958].

"Image Archive on the American Eugenics Movement." Dolan DNA Learning Center, Cold Spring Harbor Laboratory, Cold Spring Harbor, NY. Accessed December 2, 2018. http://www.eugenicsarchive.org/eugenics/list3.pl.

"Infertility FAQs." Centers for Disease Control and Prevention, April 18, 2018. https://www.cdc.gov/reproductivehealth/infertility/index.htm.

Ingham, Richard. "EUGENICS: Stupidity Should Be Cured—Watson," Darwin Awards, June 19, 2002. https://darwinawards.com/old/main200306a.html.

Inhorn, Marcia. "Making Muslim Babies: IVF and Gamete Donation in Sunni versus Shi'a Islam." *Culture, Medicine, and Psychiatry* 30 (October 2006): 427–450. http://ukpmc.ac.uk/articlerender.cgi?artid=860906.

"IVF by the Numbers." Penn Medicine, Fertility Blog, March 14, 2018. https://www.pennmedicine.org/updates/blogs/fertility-blog/2018/march/ivf-by-the-numbers.

"IVF Mix-up Heads for Court." BBC News, July 8, 2002. http://news.bbc.co.uk/2/hi/health/2115522.stm.

"IVF Under the Microscope." BBC News, July 8, 2002. http://news.bbc.co.uk/2/hi/health/2115741.stm.

Jacoby, Jeff. "Choosing to Eliminate Unwanted Daughters." *Boston Globe*, April 6, 2008. https://www.boston.com/bostonglobe/editorial_opinion/oped/articles/2008/04/06/choosing_to_eliminate_unwanted_daughters.

Jadva, Vasanti, et al. "The Experiences of Adolescents and Adults Conceived by Sperm Donation: Comparisons by Age of Disclosure and Family Type." *Human Reproduction* 24 (2009): 1909–1919. http://humrep.oxfordjournals.org/cgi/content/abstract/24/8/1909.

Johnson, Carolyn Y. "Chinese Scientist's Claim of Gene-Edited Babies Creates Uproar." *Washington Post*, November 26, 2018. https://www.washingtonpost.com/science/2018/11/26/scientists-claim-gene-edited-babies-creates-uproar/?utm_term=.f85d80fcd2d7.

Johnson, Kate. "ASRM: Pressure Builds for Open-Identity Sperm Donation in the U.S." *MedPage Today*, November 14, 2008. http://www.medpagetoday.com/MeetingCoverage/ASRM/11783.

Jones Institute for Reproductive Medicine. http://www.jonesinstitute.org.

Kahn, Susan Martha. *Reproducing Jews: A Cultural Account of Assisted Conception in Israel (Body, Commodity, Text)*. Chapel Hill, NC: Duke University Press, 2000.

Kass, Leon, and James Q. Wilson. *The Ethics of Human Cloning*. Washington, DC: The AEI Press, 1998.

Katz, Neil. "Abortion in India: Selecting by Gender." *Washington Post*, May 20, 2006. http://www.washingtonpost.com/wp-dyn/content/article/2006/05/19/AR2006051901219.html.

Keown, Damien. "'No Harm' Applies to Stem Cell Embryos: One Buddhist's View." *Science and Theology News* (April 2004). http://www.beliefnet.com/News/Science-Religion/2004/04/No-Harm-Applies-To-Stem-Cell-Embryos-One-Buddhists-View.aspx.

Kessel, Michelle, and Jessica Hopper. "Victims Speak Out about North Carolina Sterilization Program, Which Targeted Women, Young Girls and Blacks." NBC News, November 7, 2011. http://rockcenter.nbcnews.com/_news/2011/11/07/8640744-victims-speak-out-about-north-carolina-sterilization-program-which-targeted-women-young-girls-and-blacks.

Kevles, Daniel. *In the Name of Eugenics: Genetics and the Uses of Human Heredity*. New York: Alfred Knopf, 1985.

Khamsi, Roxanne. "Children with Gene Disorder Share Sperm Donor Dad." *New Scientist*, May 23, 2006. http://www.newscientist.com/article/dn9208-children-with-gene-disorder-share-sperm-donor-dad.html.

Klein, Wendy. *Building a Better Race: Gender, Sexuality, and Eugenics from the Turn of the Century to the Baby Boom*. Berkeley, CA: University of California Press, 2001.

Klitzman, Robert, et al. "Preimplantation Genetic Diagnosis on In Vitro Fertilization Clinic Websites: Presentations of Risks, Benefits, and Other Information." *Fertility and Sterility* 92 (October

2009): 1276–1283. http://www.fertstert.org/article/S00150282(08)03298-6/abstract.

Ko, Lisa. "Unwanted Sterilization and Eugenics Programs in the United States." PBS, January 29, 2016. http://www.pbs.org/independentlens/blog/unwanted-sterilization-and-eugenics-programs-in-the-united-states.

Kodjak, Alison. "Trump Admin Will Protect Health Workers Who Refuse Services on Religious Grounds." NPR, January 18, 2018. https://www.npr.org/sections/health-shots/2018/01/18/578811426/trump-will-protect-health-workers-who-reject-patients-on-religious-grounds.

Kohl, Beth. *Embryo Culture: Making Babies in the Twenty-First Century.* New York: Farrar, Straus, and Giroux, 2007.

Kolata, Gina. "Scientists Bypass Need for Embryo to Get Stem Cells." *New York Times*, November 21, 2007. http://www.nytimes.com/2007/11/21/science/21stem.html?_r=1.

Krieger, Liz. "Everything You Need to Know About Surrogacy." *Harper's Bazaar*, November 20, 2017. https://www.harpersbazaar.com/celebrity/latest/a12008347/surrogate-pregnancy-facts-cost.

Kühl, Stefan. *The Nazi Connection: Eugenics, American Racism, and German National Socialism.* Oxford, UK: Oxford University Press, 1994.

Kuntz, Dieter. *Deadly Medicine: Creating the Master Race.* Washington, DC: United States Holocaust Memorial Museum, 2004.

Landau, Ruth, and Ruth Weissenberg. "Disclosure of Donor Conception in Single-Mother Families: Views and Concerns." *Human*

Reproduction 25 (2010): 942–948. http://humrep.oxfordjournals.org/cgi/content/abstract/25/4/942.

Lawson, Dominic. "Of Course a Deaf Couple Want a Deaf Child." *London Independent*, March 11, 2008.

Lehrman, Sally. "Dolly's Creator Moves Away from Cloning and Embryonic Stem Cells." *Scientific American*, August 2008. http://www.scientificamerican.com/article.cfm?id=no-more-cloning-around.

Levine, Aaron. "Self-Regulation, Compensation, and the Ethical Recruitment of Oocyte Donors." *Hastings Center Report* 40 (March/April 2010): 25–36. http://www.thehastingscenter.org/Publications/ HCR/Detail.aspx?id=4549.

Lombardo, Paul. *Three Generations, No Imbeciles: Eugenics, the Supreme Court, and Buck v. Bell.* Baltimore: Johns Hopkins University Press, 2008.

"Male Infertility." US Department of Health and Human Services. Accessed November 29, 2018. https://www.hhs.gov/opa/reproductive-health/fact-sheets/female-infertility/index.html.

Malisow, Craig. "Donor Babies Search for Their Anonymous Fathers." *Houston Press*, November 6, 2008. http://www.houstonpress.com/2008-11-06/news/donor-babies-search-for-their-anonymous-fathers/1.

Malvern, Jack. "Sperm Donor Forced to Pay Child Support After Lesbian Couple Split." *London Times*, December 4, 2007. http://women.timesonline.co.uk/tol/life_and_style/women/families/article2994783.ece.

Mamdani, Bashir. "In Support of Sex Selection." *Indian Journal of Medical Ethics* 28 (2002): 335–336.

Marcus, Ruth. "I Would've Aborted a Fetus with Down Syndrome. Women Need That Right." *Washington Post*, March 9, 2018. https://www.washingtonpost.com/opinions/i-wouldve-aborted-a-fetus-with-down-syndrome-women-need-that-right/2018/03/09/3aaac364-23d6-11e8-94da-ebf9d112159c_story.html?utm_term=.a7426416ca6e.

Miah, Andy. *Genetically Modified Athletes: Biomedical Ethics, Gene Doping, and Sport*. London: Routledge, 2004.

Mick, Hayley. "Contact with Donor Siblings a Good Experience for Most Families." *Globe and Mail* (Canada), February 26, 2009. http://www.theglobeandmail.com/life/article973923.ece.

Minkel, J. "Korean Cloned Human Cells Were Product of 'Virgin Birth.'" *Scientific American*, August 2, 2007. http://www.scientificamerican.com/article.cfm?id=korean-cloned-human-cells.

Moreton, Cole. "World's First Test-Tube Baby Louise Brown Has a Child of Her Own." (London) *Independent*, January 14, 2007. http://www.independent.co.uk/life-style/health-and-families/health-news/worlds-first-testtube-baby-louise-brown-has-a-child-of-her-own-432080.html.

———. "My Scattered Grandchildren." *Globe and Mail*, September 13, 2009. http://www.theglobeandmail.com/life/family-and-relationships/my-scattered-grandchildren/article1286201.

Motluk, Alison. “Anonymous Sperm Donor Traced on Internet.” *New Scientist*, November 3, 2005. http://www.newscientist.com/article/mg18825244.200-anonymous-sperm-donor-traced-on-internet.html.

Mundy, Liza. *Everything Conceivable: How Assisted Reproduction Is Changing Men, Women, and the World*. New York: Alfred Knopf, 2007.

Naff, Clay, ed. *Reproductive Technologies*. Detroit: Greenhaven Press, 2007.

Neil, Martha. “Court Says Sperm Donor Owes Child Support.” *American Bar Association Journal*, May 10, 2007. http://www.abajournal.com/news/article/court-says-sperm-donor-owes-child-support.

“New Donor Registrations.” Human Fertilisation and Embryology Authority, July 21, 2009. http://www.hfea.gov.uk/3411.html.

New Oxford Annotated Bible, New Revised Standard Version, 3rd ed. Oxford, UK: Oxford University Press, 2007.

“Obama’s Stem Cell Policy Hasn’t Reversed Legislative Restrictions.” Fox News, March 14, 2009. http://www.foxnews.com/politics/2009/03/14/obamas-stem-cell-policy-reversed-legislative-restrictions.

“One in Five Pregnancies Worldwide Ends in Abortion, Study Says.” Fox News, October 12, 2007. http://www.foxnews.com/story/0,2933,301370,00.html.

“On This Day: 25 July 1978—First Test-Tube Baby Born.” BBC News. Accessed December 2, 2018. http://news.bbc.co.uk/onthisday/hi/dates/stories/july/25/newsid_2499000/2499411.stm.

Parfit, Derek. *Reasons and Persons*. Oxford, UK: Clarendon Press, 1984.

Picoult, Jodi. *My Sister's Keeper*. New York: Washington Square Press, 2005.

Plaut, W. Gunther, ed. *The Torah: A Modern Commentary*. New York: Union of American Hebrew Congregations, 1981.

Pollack, Andrew. "Awaiting the Genome Payoff." *New York Times*, June 15, 2010. https://www.nytimes.com/2010/06/15/business/15genome.html.

Poore, Michael. "Baby Shopping: The Clash of Worldviews in Bioethics." Humanitas Project, April 2007. http://www.humanitas.org/articles/babyshopping.htm.

Pope Paul VI. "Encyclical Letter Humanae Vitae of the Supreme Pontiff Paul VI … on the Regulation of Birth." Vatican, July 25, 1968. https://w2.vatican.va/content/paul-vi/en/encyclicals/documents/hf_p-vi_enc_25071968_humanae-vitae.html.

Ramsey, Paul. *Fabricated Man: The Ethics of Genetic Control*. New Haven, CT: Yale University Press, 1970.

Ratzinger, Joseph, and Alberto Bovone. "Respect for Human Life: Congregation for the Doctrine of the Faith." Eternal Word Television Network, February 1987. http://www.ewtn.com/library/curia/cdfhuman.htm.

Raymond, Janice. *Women as Wombs: Reproductive Technologies and the Battle over Women's Freedom*. San Francisco: Harper, 1993.

Reilly, Philip. *The Surgical Solution: A History of Involuntary Sterilization in the United States*. Baltimore: Johns Hopkins University Press, 1991.

Roberts, Sam. "U.S. Births Hint at Bias for Boys in Some Asians." *New York Times*, June 14, 2009. https://www.nytimes.com/2009/06/15/nyregion/15babies.html.

Sandel, Michael. *The Case Against Perfection: Ethics in the Age of Genetic Engineering*. Cambridge, MA: Belknap Press, 2007.

Savulescu, Julian. "Deaf Lesbians, 'Designer Disability,' and the Future of Medicine." *British Medical Journal* 325 (October 5, 2002): 771–773. http://www.ncbi.nlm.nih.gov/pmc/articles/PMC1124279.

Sawyer, Neroli. "Sperm Donor Limits that Control for the 'Relative' Risk Associated with the Use of Open-Identity Donors." *Human Reproduction* 25 (2010): 1089–1096. http://humrep.oxfordjournals.org/cgi/content/abstract/25/5/1089.

Schneider, Angela, and Theodore Friedmann. *Gene Doping in Sports: The Science and Ethics of Genetically Modified Athletes*. Boston: Elsevier, 2006.

Scully, Jackie. *Disability Bioethics: Moral Bodies, Moral Difference*. Lanham, MD: Rowman and Littlefield, 2008.

Seng, S., et al. "In-Vitro Fertilisation in Women Aged 40 Years and Above." *Singapore Medical Journal* 46 (March 2005): 132–136. http://www.sma.org.sg/smj/smjmainpges/4603main.html.

Sheldon, S., and S. Wilkinson. "Should Selecting Saviour Siblings Be Banned?" *Journal of Medical Ethics* 30 (December 2004): 533–537. http://www.ncbi.nlm.nih.gov/pmc/articles/PMC1733988.

Siddiqi, Muzammil. "An Islamic Perspective on Stem Cells Research." Islam 101, 2001. http://www.islam101.com/science/stemCells.htm.

Smith, Rebecca. "Sperm Donors Should Get Cut-Price IVF to Tackle Shortage." *Telegraph* (London), November 11, 2008. http://www.telegraph.co.uk/health/healthnews/3439954/Sperm-donors-should-get-cut-price-IVF-to-tackle-shortage.html.

Spar, Debora. *The Baby Business: How Money, Science, and Politics Drive the Commerce of Conception*. Boston: Harvard Business School Press, 2006.

"Sperm Donor Shortage Hits Canadian Infertility Clinics." CBC News, December 19, 2006. http://www.cbc.ca/health/story/2006/12/19/sperm-shortage.html.

Spriggs, M., and Julian Savulescu. "Saviour Siblings." *Journal of Medical Ethics* 28 (October 2002): 289.

Springen, Karen. "What It Means to Be a Woman." *Newsweek*, September 15, 2008.

Squire, Alison. "A Generation of Sperm Donor Children Are Discovering the Father They Know and Love Is NOT Their Father at All." *Daily Mail*, March 19, 2009. http://www.dailymail.co.uk/femail/article-1163032/A-generation-sperm-donor-children-discovering-father-know-love-NOT-father-all.html.

"Statistics." Parkinson's Foundation. Accessed November 30, 2018. https://parkinson.org/Understanding-Parkinsons/Causes-and-Statistics/Statistics.

Steinbock, Bonnie. "Preventing Sex-Selective Abortions in America: A Solution in Search of a Problem." Hastings Center, April 4, 2017. https://www.thehastingscenter.org/preventing-sex-selective-abortions-america-solution-search-problem.

"Stem Cell Research." Religious Action Center of Reform Judaism, July 26, 2005. http://rac.org/advocacy/issues/stemcell/#rjm.

Stepan, Nancy. *'The Hour of Eugenics': Race, Gender, and Nation in Latin America*. Ithaca, New York: Cornell University Press, 1991.

Stewart, Lorna. "Is the Human Embryo Sacrosanct? Gamete Donation and Doctrine." *BioNews* 490 (January 2009). http://www.bionews.org.uk/page_13633.asp.

"Sweden Rules 'Gender-Based' Abortion Legal." *Local* (Sweden), May 12, 2009. http://www.thelocal.se/19392/20090512/.

Syed, Fatima. "Disappearing Girls of India." *Pakistan Observer*, November 5, 2009.

Tatlow, Didi Kirsten. "In China, a Lonely Valentine's Day for Millions of Men." *New York Times*, February 14, 2017. https://www.nytimes.com/2017/02/14/world/asia/china-men-marriage-gender-gap.html.

Tuller, David. "Payment Offers to Egg Donors Prompt Scrutiny." *New York Times*, May 11, 2010. https://www.nytimes.com/2010/05/11/health/11eggs.html.

"2006 Assisted Reproductive Technology (ART) Report: Commonly Asked Questions." Centers for Disease Control and Prevention, 2006. http://www.cdc.gov/ART/ART2006/faq.htm#1.

"2006 Assisted Reproductive Technology (ART) Report: Section 5—ART Trends, 1996–2006." Centers for Disease Control and Prevention, 2006. http://www.cdc.gov/ART/ART2006/section5.htm.

"Union of Orthodox Jewish Congregations Welcomes U.S. House Passage of Stem Cell Research Enhancement Act." Institute for Public Affairs, May 25, 2005. http://www.ou.org/public/statements/2005/n11.htm.

Urofsky, Melvin, and Paul Finkelman. *Documents of American Constitutional and Legal History*. New York: Oxford University Press, 2002.

"U.S. Fertility Market to Gain Nearly $1B over Next 5 Years." BCC Research, January 11, 2018. https://www.bccresearch.com/pressroom/hlc/us-fertility-market-to-gain-nearly-$1b-over-next-5-years.

Wagner, Viqi, ed. *Biomedical Ethics*. Detroit, MI: Greenhaven Press, 2008.

Wahrman, Miryam. "Assisted Reproduction and Judaism." Jewish Virtual Library. Accessed December 2, 2018. https://www.jewishvirtuallibrary.org/assisted-reproduction-and-judaism.

Washington, Samantha. "Secret World of Sperm Donations." BBC, September 18, 2009. http://news.bbc.co.uk/2/hi/uk_news/8261034.stm.

Weil, Elizabeth. "A Wrongful Birth." *New York Times*, March 12, 2006. http://www.nytimes.com/2006/03/12/magazine/312wrongful.1.html.

"Well-Paid Sperm Donations Up During Slumping Economy." WCBD Charleston, SC, April 6, 2009. http://www2.counton2.com/cbd/news/money_squeeze/article/well-paid_sperm_donations_up_during_slumping_economy/23190.

"What Did Pope Francis Actually Say About Contraception?" Catholic News Agency, February 18, 2016. https://www.catholicnewsagency.com/news/what-did-pope-francis-actually-say-about-contraception-47196.

Whitehouse, Beth. *The Match: 'Savior Siblings' and One Family's Battle to Heal Their Daughter.* Boston: Beacon Press, 2010.

Williams, Chris. "Stem Cell Fraudster Made 'Virgin Birth' Breakthrough." *Register,* August 3, 2007. www.theregister.co.uk/2007/08/03/hwang_parthenogenesis.

"Woman Loses Final Embryo Appeal." BBC News, April 10, 2007. http://news.bbc.co.uk/2/hi/health/6530295.stm.

"Woman Loses Frozen Embryos Fight." BBC News, March 7, 2006. http://news.bbc.co.uk/2/hi/health/4779876.stm.

Wooden, Cindy. "Global Catholic Population Tops 1.28 Billion; Half Are in 10 Countries." *National Catholic Reporter,* April 8, 2017. https://www.ncronline.org/news/world/global-catholic-population-tops-128-billion-half-are-10-countries.

Zhuang, Pinghui. "End of China's One Child Policy Sees Births Rise to 18.46 Million in 2016 ... but It's Still Not Enough." *South China Morning Post,* January 23, 2017. https://www.scmp.com/news/china/policies-politics/article/2064580/end-chinas-one-child-policy-sees-births-rise-1846.

Zitner, Aaron. "A Girl or Boy, You Pick." *Los Angeles Times,* July 23, 2002. http://www.geneticsandsociety.org/article.php?id=105.

Index

About the Authors

Erin L. McCoy is a literature, language, and cultural studies educator and an award-winning photojournalist and poet. She holds a master of arts degree in Hispanic studies and a master of fine arts degree in creative writing from the University of Washington. She has edited more than two dozen nonfiction books for young adults, including *The Mexican-American War*, *The Israel-Palestine Border Conflict*, and *Poverty: Public Crisis or Private Struggle?* from Cavendish Square Publishing. She is from Louisville, Kentucky.

Jon Sterngass is a writer specializing in children's nonfiction who has written more than forty books. Born and raised in Brooklyn, Sterngass holds a bachelor of arts degree from Franklin and Marshall College, a master of arts in medieval history from the University of Wisconsin–Milwaukee, and a PhD from the City University of New York in nineteenth-century American history.